The Rich Housewife (A Gripping Psychological Thriller with a Shocking Twist)

Ann-Marie Richards

Published by Ann-Marie Richards, 2020.

THE RICH HOUSEWIFE
(A gripping psychological thriller with a shocking twist)
by Ann-Marie Richards

This is a work of fiction. Similarities to real people, places, or events are entirely coincidental.

THE RICH HOUSEWIFE (A GRIPPING PSYCHOLOGICAL THRILLER WITH A SHOCKING TWIST)

First edition. June 12, 2020.

ISBN: 978-1393263500

Written by Ann-Marie Richards.

Acknowledgement
Thank you to my amazing Father, my amazing family and friends and to my wonderful editor Phyllis.

RAVE REVIEWS
for
MISSING
(A gripping psychological thriller with a shocking twist)
By Ann-Marie Richards

"I did not expect this story to end so dramatically. Very twisted conclusion. That being said, the story was riveting and I had trouble putting it down . Very good read." -(Review on Amz)

"I couldn't put the book down . I was so surprised at the end . I enjoyed very much. Thanks" -(Review on Amz)

"Wow! What a twist!!! Loved this story. I did not see that twist coming." -(Review on Goodreads)

"I love, love, love the twist at the end." -(ARC reviewer)

"A very well written psychological thriller..."-(Review on Amz)

"Excellent read. I was completely unprepared for the ending!! It was like a thrilling rollercoaster ride with

all the twists and turns of a gripping psychological thriller!!" –(Review on Amz)

"Wow!! To say the book kept you on your toes is an understatement!!! Mind boggling and very suspenseful."- (Review on Amz)

"Wow! I was fooled until the very end! I couldn't stop reading!" -(Review on Goodreads)

"What a twist!" -(Review on Goodreads)

"Couldn't put the book down. Had to read one more chapter. Great twist at the end. Loved it." –(Review on Kobo)

"Thrilling!"

"Probably one of the best I've read lately!" -(Review on Amz)

"Absolutely loved this one!" -(Review on Amz)

"Excellent! Another great read!" -(Review on Amz)

THE RICH HOUSEWIFE

Some people will stop at nothing to get what they want...

Formerly homeless hustler Bianca Thomson-Wingarden had it all planned out. She found a rich man to get her pregnant and marry so she could give her child a lavish life of financial security she'd carefully prepared for.

She and her new husband Elvin Wingarden III, heir to the Wingarden billion-dollar dynasty, have the perfect life. They split their time between their upscale condo in the city and their lavish 17-bedroom mansion in the country. They drive the latest luxury vehicles. They don't have to worry about money and she can shower their daughter Evie, their little dog, and their friends with everything they desire.

The trouble is, their perfect life is about to fall apart. Elvin is no longer the charming man she married. And when Elvin's mother decides to hire the mysterious Penny as a live-in nanny to help take care of little Evie, everything starts going wrong in Bianca's life. She gets a terrible suspicion that the new nanny is there to replace her. And why does that nanny look so familiar?

A thrilling suspense filled with dark family secrets, popularity contests, and deception.

Peniaphobia:
The intense fear of poverty, fear of being broke, fear of being poor, fear of having no money. Fear of not being able to survive.
For some people, the fear is so intense they will stop at nothing to avoid it.
But as the saying goes, be careful what you wish for.

"All that glisters is not gold"
– William Shakespeare
The Merchant of Venice, 1596

1. Bianca

Bianca's list for how to secure a rich husband
One must...

1. *Be charming and outgoing. Be a good listener.*
2. *Keep up appearances. Have regular facials, expensive mani-pedis, styled hair, stylish clothes, massages, wear shape-flattering expensive clothing over exotic lingerie.*
3. *Keep in top shape. Work out at the gym or exercise at home but adhere to a 1500 calorie-a-day diet. Practice hot yoga.*
4. *Have appreciation for the finer things in life such as spa treatments, haute cuisine, luxury cars, rare diamonds, fine artwork, art galleries, gourmet cooking classes, theatre, etc.*
5. *Educate yourself on current world events. It helps to know what's going on in the world to carry on an intellectually-stimulating conversation*
6. *Make a difference. Do volunteer work or be engaged with a popular foundation. One MUST have a cause or charity focus to show that you care about something in this world other than oneself.*
7. *Attend upscale functions, such as events at prestigious clubs, sports events, and elite restaurants that the affluent are likely to frequent.*
8. *Be creative and innovative in the bedroom at providing and receiving stimulating sexual pleasures that will blow his mind.*

Somebody was out to get Bianca Thomson-Wingarden.

Who on earth found this list and placed it in Bianca's notebook planner? Was it Vera, her mother-in-law?

It must have been. Who else would it be?

That woman was always sneaking around, listening to calls and spying on people.

Vera had been out to get Bianca from day one.

Bianca's lungs squeezed, her eyes widened in shock as she held the piece of paper that she'd stuck in her diary and hid in the attic after marrying Elvin.

She always thought if anyone saw this list, she'd be dead. It was meant to be a joke, but her husband might not think so. Bianca ran her fingers over the note.

She sat in her study with the sun shining in through the floor-to-ceiling windows overlooking a breathtaking view of their private lake, unsure how to handle this.

She was going to pretend she never saw it. It was typed, thank goodness. No one could prove she wrote it.

Besides, she thought to herself while sliding the paper into the shredder beside the oak desk in her office at the mansion, she had to make some more calls relating to her daughter Evie's upcoming fourth birthday. She didn't have time for this crap.

She'd never known what it was like to have birthday parties growing up. Every year until she ran away, she has been in a foster home. She'd never had the luck of sticking around long enough for anyone to throw her a party. Still, she was glad to have the right father for her baby: one of the richest men in the country.

Some may call her a gold digger. But she was not. Not even close. She was just a girl with goals. A *goal* digger who had big goals to dig herself out of an impoverished, traumatic past. She worked hard and only wanted to have a decent life for her and her child, not like the life she grew up with. But that was in her past now. No one need know about that. It was buried and gone.

Buried in the past.

Right now, she had a new role to play, that of a good housewife to a man born into a wealthy, philanthropic family.

If her mother in-law was trying to frighten her away, it wasn't working. The family wouldn't be able to stand a divorce. They knew it. And she had given them the only heir to the Wingarden dynasty, since her husband could not have more children since the accident.

Yet she had to keep watch over her shoulder and behind her back. No enemy could ever hurt her as much as someone close to her. She knew that enemies couldn't betray you, only someone you already trusted.

Trust no one.

And right now, jealousy lurked in her inner circle. Someone was out to get her. But who? And why? Being rich came with a lot of baggage. There were lots of people who wanted to knock you down.

She'd been getting a lot of cold stares from members of the staff and frosty vibes from Vera Wingarden, Elvin's mother, who still roamed the mansion since her husband, Elvin the second, had passed away.

A smirk curved her cherry-red, lipstick-covered lips. She was not giving in that easily. They were not getting rid of her. She knew too much about them. She'd hustled her way to get to where she was and she wasn't going out without a fight.

This morning she'd been listed as the richest housewife in SunValley, Ontario. Heck, she was one of the richest housewives in the country according to *Forbella Magazine*. She was head of several fundraising organizations that served the purpose of raising her popularity online. She just reached twenty million followers on her social media accounts. The board of directors loved her.

They can't get rid of me that easily.

Even if they checked her background, which she was sure they would have done by now, it was too late. She was the mother of the heir. Nothing they could do about it now.

Elvin wouldn't dare do anything that could cost him half his fortune in a divorce. Would he?

Still, she was in their rich inner circle now.

She was the woman of the house, or the queen of this mansion that had been built in 1909 by Elvin the first who founded the Wingarden Department Store. Of course, life had been better for the retailer before the current changing markets and online shopping that proved to be a struggle. Most of the newest breed of billionaires were in the tech industry.

Still, the Wingarden mansion, a symbol of 'old' money, with its extravagantly done interiors was impressive, boasting 17 bedrooms, 22 bathrooms, 19 fireplaces, and cavernous spaces for entertaining guests, a 16-car garage, 2 vodka bars, and a massive home theatre in addition to three children's Disney-themed play areas and two tricked out nurseries.

One of the drawing rooms had its original painted ceiling. They had a tennis court, four massive formal gardens, an indoor swimming pool with spa and a beautifully-designed outdoor swimming pool where they hosted pool parties while she wore her $15,000 designer dresses. The Wingarden family had over twenty million followers on social media, thanks in part to Bianca's social skills and ability to capture every lavish moment to share with followers.

Her baby bump and pregnancy pics were her most popular to date. Everyone loved babies and especially rich babies who were heir to massive fortunes. Evie was a star from birth. Unlike the life Bianca'd had when her own mother abandoned her at birth and ran off, leaving her father to raise her until he died when she was seven.

That's in the past now, Bianca. Let it go.

Vera Wingarden, widow of Elvin II, lived with them. In fact, Elvin III had never moved out. Bianca had to work around that and luckily, she could keep out of Vera's way most of the time. But Vera seemed to keep a close watch at all times over her son, granddaughter and Bianca. Vera called the shots where finances were concerned, but Bianca was going to make sure that changed soon.

The Wingarden Mansion presided over 32 breathtaking acres of forest and formal gardens.

It would kill Elvin and his mother to have to split the property in two.

Didn't matter that they couldn't stand each other.

Before meeting Elvin, Bianca had been struggling, working two mundane jobs, waitressing at a café that rich men frequented, wearing the tightest black form-hugging dress to work, per the dress code, serving the wealthy, while scanning for an opportunity to get out of the low-paying rat race, competing for the best tables and tips, working on her feet in painful heels while being watched by her employer, unable to take a bathroom break when she needed.

That was her old life.

She'd grown up so poor, she often skipped lunch because her dad couldn't afford to pack any for her. She was through with being poor. It wasn't fair. Both of her parents had been poor and neither could do anything for their child. Her mother should have married well. Bianca wouldn't have grown up the way she had with nothing if her mother had married well.

So she'd decided to marry rich to become rich. As long as she did her part and provided an heir.

There was nothing she wouldn't do to have it all.

Nothing.

She wondered what her mother-in-law would say if she knew about her real background.

Bianca got up from her plush leather executive chair and went to the study area and moved a portrait on the wall to the side to open the safe hidden behind it. The home had many safes. This was her own. She then placed another note inside it and locked the door, closing it and winding the safe dial. She then moved the portrait back into place.

Vera and her friend, Gossiping Gloria had looked down at her when she accompanied Elvin to a gala event. They'd whispered about Bianca being a gold digger. Well, she showed them. So far, she'd done her part and played her role perfectly in the public eye. Bianca had it all planned out. She was the perfect wife.

Her mind drifted to the time when she'd spotted Elvin III while scanning the Changee's Club, an upscale pick-up joint near the financial district that had been a hot spot since the early 1970s.

Well, they didn't actually call it a pick-up joint. It was one of those unwritten social expectations. Dinner, drinks and dance, then a private suite. That's what it was all about at Changee's. A club tailored to those who expected nothing but the best. The finest, most expensive wine and cuisine, private lounges. Celebrations with champagne, cognac and brandy sometimes followed by a little fooling around.

She was there to meet some friends, maybe interview for a job as a wait staff. Her nerves got the best of her. Could she really do this?

The atmosphere was pumping and high energy music coursed through the place.

Women dressed in tight little black dresses that accentuated their assets: tiny waists, big boobs, and rounded butts. And those were the waitresses and some of the bottle service staff, never mind the female clientele. Sometimes bottles of the finest could cost $600 or more for a client who could drop hundred-dollar bills like pennies in a well.

The men dressed to impress to show *their* assets—their wallets. They liked it when the women flirted with them and whispered in their ear they'd perform anything they wanted upstairs in one of the private suites.

The women at Changee's Club were hired for their looks as well as their abilities. The two went hand in hand. If they didn't look like a Kardashian, they probably wouldn't make the cut to the next stage of the interview, which was in violation of labor laws. Of course, they wouldn't tell this to the applicants.

She was *not* a gold digger. She was a goal digger. She was woman who needed to achieve her goals in life by exchanging favors with another. She was a woman who wanted to get the most out of life in exchange for something else. What was so bad about that? She wasn't a bad person. She was just a person who'd been a victim of bad circumstances and wanted a better life.

She wasn't engaging in anything nefarious.

Then again, people were often blind to their own faults. It was something to do with an ego defence mechanism.

She tried using her brains and didn't get anywhere except an overpriced rental without rent control and a crazy roommate. A mountain of student debt and no job to pay it off.

She was going to use her womb. Her former roommate once told her, you need a room and a womb.

That roommate got knocked up by a rich, married guy. She didn't feel bad about it and said that if he were stupid enough to cheat on his wife and on top of that not use a condom, then he got what he deserved. Bianca didn't agree with her roommate then, but then things changed.

A baby would change everything.

A baby would be her ticket to freedom.

Her ticket out of poverty. Her way out. Her means to support herself. She was after the big ticket. Child support payments. One woman she read about was getting $100,000 a month from some real estate mogul. Another former waitress received $50,000 a month in child support payments from a movie star.

Bianca always dreamed that would be her life.

She might not be a perfect person, but she wanted to have the best in life. She was through with struggling and yes, her mission was to land a good man.

Marry rich.

Or get knocked up by a rich man.

She had often overheard conversations at work from hot waitresses looking to trick rich men into having unprotected sex with them.

Everyone needs financial security these days.

It was part of a piranha culture.

One girl told her she was going to get married to a very rich dude soon. That was her retirement plan. Her *career* plan. "The easiest way to get rich is to marry a rich guy," the girl had told her that night, "You do that by getting pregnant. Then he'll have no choice but to marry you or pay up in massive child support."

"Rich men are the easiest targets," the woman had said. "Nothing wrong with wanting to live a comfortable life and afford to take care of your children, is there?"

The girl then went on to tell her she was sick of living with low standards. She wanted a good home to bring up her children and to eat expensive, wonderful meals every day. She wanted to be surrounded by beautiful things. She wanted designer clothes and handbags and shoes, exotic holidays in five-star hotels abroad. She wanted a wealthy older man with confidence, stability and security. One who'd played out his playing days and wanted to stay home at night and pamper and spend time with his woman. His *one* woman.

Another workmate had boasted that she was going to retire from waitressing early and reinvent herself and marry a rich man and live a lavish lifestyle, being served instead of serving others, go on skiing trips, dining in the finest restaurants, drinking the finest champagnes and not having to work awful unsociable hours ever again or worry how to pay rent if you've missed work because you were sick with the flu for two weeks.

At first, Bianca was sickened by what women like that were doing, but then she gave it a good, long thought. They were just matchmaking on their own. It wasn't as if they didn't take care of their husbands or make them happy or do whatever they wanted for them, right? No one was forcing them to have sex with them, right?

Wrong. Wrong. Wrong.

But no matter how many times she told herself it was wrong. Being broke, penniless and homeless didn't feel exactly *right*, did it?

She wasn't a gold digger but a goal digger. She wanted to have a better life for her children. She didn't want them to do without.

Everything cost money. Inflation and salaries were not compatible. In her folks' day, stuff lasted forever. Now you have to keep buying phones because they don't work after a few years or technology is not built to last or changes often. Who could afford this? Not to mention if an emergency comes up. Then what?

No, it took money to get things gone.

Food, water and shelter wasn't free in the western world. And those were the fundamental items for survival. She was a survivor. So what if she married rich so her kids could have everything they needed?

Bianca's thoughts were soon interrupted by the doors to the study sliding open followed and the sound of hard heels on the marble floor.

It was her monster-in-law.

"My dear," Vera said, clasping her hands together.

Did she ever call her Bianca?

"Yes Ma'am?" Bianca was told to always address Vera as Ma'am.

"We were just thinking about your commitments."

"My commitments?"

"Yes, dear. With all the events coming up and your calendar getting busy, you hardly have time for Evie and all the other things you're required to do. You haven't been able to attend as many functions this year and that's not acceptable. People will begin to talk."

"It's been tiring looking after Evie. She has a lot of energy."

They'd gone through tons of nannies with large boobs, ogling her husband. Bianca got rid of them fast. Her husband seemed to hate her more for that. But if she were being honest to herself, looking after her energetic, smart preschooler wasn't a walk in the park. Dark circles had started to show under her eyes, which makeup did little to hide. She noticed it when she'd taken a selfie at one of the gala events.

Bianca had almost forgotten that there was a price to pay for being a rich housewife in the Wingarden household. Image was everything. It wasn't enough to be successful, one had to *appear* successful in every way. And in a time where retail department stores filed for bankruptcy and other long-time retailers fell victim to the online marketplace, they had to prove they were resilient, though they hadn't kept up with the times as much as they should have.

The elder Elvin II hadn't kept up very well and hoped his lazy son Elvin III would do something, but he failed, too, which was why the bitter Elvin II, Bianca's late father-in-law, on his deathbed said he would leave everything to charity as his stocks declined, not to his high-spending son or his widow. But when he learned Elvin III was having a child, he had a change of heart and said half would go to his grandchild in the hopes that the grandchildren would have better business sense than their father.

"What are you suggesting, Ma'am?" Bianca asked politely, scooping up Porsche, her two-year old Yorkshire Terrier, who'd just trotted into the study. Her little Yorkie was a cute bundle of joy and never had public tantrums like her three-year old human child—what a temperament, just like her father. Still, she tried to be patient with her since she was the heir.

Porsche was a gift from one of their associates. Bianca loved stroking Porsche's silky coat. Porsche always got tons of likes on her social media page, everyone melted at her adorable selfies with Porsche.

Good thing she didn't have to lift a finger to take care of her. Porsche had her own dog-groomer who did everything. The groomer fed Porsche gourmet dog food three times a day, exercised her twice a day, bathed her, blow dried her silky coat of fur, and spend ages brushing it out, adding silky diamond embroidered decorative bow to her top knot.

"Since you have so much on your to-do list, it would be proper to have a little help with Evie, especially with the race coming up soon, not to mention you need to get her ready for her preschool entrance exam."

Evie was about to take her entrance exam for one of the most elite private schools in the country. A school that accepted only little geniuses.

"Yes, I supposed I could use some extra help."

It had been months since she fired the last nanny. Vera and Elvin were not pleased. Truth be told, she thought they'd hired the nanny as a spy.

Yes, it would be wonderful to have a little help with Evie again just as she had help with Porsche. That would free her to do other mind-numbing chores for the Wingarden family and to keep up with her social media posts.

Vera wore the pants in the family, since Elvin lived with her. Bianca had thought it was the other way around at first. But Elvin III was just a namesake. His late daddy had the big bucks and was an eccentric man with eccentric habits, especially where money was concerned.

Sure, they kept the mansion after his passing, but he left them nothing else and it would all go to charity unless his son could produce an heir because he trusted neither his widow nor his son. So Bianca gave him an heir. His family had hoped he'd breed with aristocratic blood but they settled for Bianca.

"How many hours a week are you thinking, Ma'am?"

Vera hesitated for a moment, playing with the pearl necklace around her neck. That annoyed Bianca to no end, she'd fantasized about tightening the beads around her neck so she wouldn't play with them again. Ever!

"I was thinking more of a live-in nanny."

Bianca froze.

She did *not* like the sound of that at all.

"A live-in nanny?" she asked incredulously.

You mean a spy to watch me and conduct herself in ways for my husband to be watching her? No thank you.

"Well, Ma'am..."

"It's not subject to negotiation." Vera's tone was sharp. "You can pick one out from the list of finalists from the agency."

A list of finalists?

Was this a beauty contest?

So Vera had gone ahead and arranged it all? As always.

Bianca's mind flickered back to the pain Vera had caused her. When she was pregnant with Evie, she told Elvin right away. Elvin said he'd marry her so Evie could be born in wedlock. But Vera was about to put a stop to it, right?

She made Bianca do an in-utero paternity test to make sure the baby was his.

Thank God it was his.

Bianca had hated her ever since, because those tests were a high risk to the fetus and the mother.

Deep breath, Bianca. Remember what you learned in hot yoga.

Bianca's palms moistened with sweat. Her heartbeat escalated. She was a nervous wreck.

This rash of events happening lately didn't help. Not to mention, appearances could be deceptive. Her mother in-law hated her, and hated the fact that she had gotten pregnant with her precious son's child.

Bianca couldn't wait for her daughter to turn four soon. She would have more access to her funds when everything was finalized, wouldn't she?

Then she'd find a way to fix Vera. To somehow ship that woman off and/or leave Elvin.

"Fine, Vera. That won't be a problem."

Bianca put up with it. For now.

She remembered overhearing conversations Vera had with her pompous society friends about Bianca's background and how she was cheapening the family name with her social media posts. But they got likes, didn't they?

There was talk about finding someone suitable for Elvin and that it wasn't too late since Elvin was secretly seeing an heiress to a European luxury vehicle company.

They wanted Bianca out of the way, didn't they?

Was Vera trying to get rid of her now that they had the heir to the Wingarden dynasty who'd inherit the billion dollar trust fund when she turned four?

There was no way Bianca was giving up all of this!

They couldn't get rid of her that easily.

Could they?

2. Bianca

An hour later, Bianca swiped the screen of the laptop computer in the French study of the manor overlooking the verdant garden and waterfall. She'd logged into the Elite Nanny Agency website with the code Vera gave her. Bianca felt helpless, locked into the rich prison of the Wingardens. She glanced in horror at the beautiful women on the screen who looked more like porn stars or supermodels, with seductive smoky eyes, full lips and beautiful hair. They were all a triple threat, because not only did they look like they'd be happy to oblige to Elvin's sexual appetite, they could do everything under the sun.

They had university degrees in early childhood education with high GPAs, black belts in Judo or other martial arts, spoke at least three or four languages including French and Spanish, they had culinary training with European chefs, and years of experience in childcare. Never mind CPR and First Aid, some of them were licensed medical professionals.

Bianca reached for her ulcer pill and popped it in her mouth then took a sip of water. The refreshing water slid down her dry throat, quenching her thirst.

Holy shit! These gorgeous women were overqualified. She didn't trust them. Not one bit.

Why hadn't they landed their own billionaires? Why do they want to play nanny for some affluent family? Was it to slide into the man of the house's bed while the wife was away?

Vera had spoken to Bianca about heading to New York by herself to attend a gathering with one of the family's investors.

She'd told Bianca it would be good to get away. Sure. And leave the sexy, hot, overqualified nanny with her husband and their three-year-old?

I don't think so.

Her heart galloped hard in her chest. Her lungs burned. She could feel her belly knot up with nerves.

Maybe that's why these women joined the elite nanny agencies for the rich, Bianca thought to herself. Anger flared inside her. And she had to choose her own replacement? She had to select from the list of finalists?

She then saw a homely girl on the last page. The woman was clearly overweight and her hair didn't shine like the others. She wasn't as qualified, but she'd taken care of the granddaughter of Lady Eloise Dartsworth, the famous European grand-duchess.

Well, that was good. She could say that Evie was being taken care of by Lady Eloise's former children's nanny?

Hmm.

The final decision was Bianca's, wasn't it?

Bianca slid her fingers across the screen and eliminated all the contestants—or the applicants, rather, and chose the homely girl. Her name was Penny. Penny the nanny.

She'd be perfect. A simple homely four-eyed twit to look after her toddler. Nothing too fancy like those other model-type boob-heavy rounded butt, masters-educated gold diggers who signed up for the elite nanny agency with one thing on their mind: to get with her crazy rich famous husband. Bianca should know. She was a gold digger once too. Though she liked the term goal digger.

3. Penny

Sweet.

Penny Andirs could not believe it. Her plan was working. The famous Wingardens wanted to hire her.

A jolt of motivation slid through Penny, the first in a long while. There was a time when she thought about giving up. But not now.

The headline of that article was scorched in Penny's brain.

The Richest Housewife in Sun Valley - Bianca Wingarden, the woman who does it all

What a fraud.

A criminal.

A con artist.

Bianca didn't deserve to be the richest housewife. Not one bit.

Fury singed Penny's blood and coursed through her veins.

Little did the Wingardens know what they would be getting themselves into. And their rich little world would be flipped upside down. Just as Penny's world had been when Bianca stole her Money.

Penny Andirs, the broke, down-and-out, debt-ridden grad with a heart-breaking past wanted *one thing* from Bianca Wingarden right now.

Penny wanted her money back, her life back, and for Bianca-not-even-her-real-name to go to prison for her horrible crime.

Okay, that was *three* things.

But still, Bianca had Penny's money. And Penny was getting her money back one way or another.

How ironic that her name was Penny. She always hated her parents for naming her after a worthless coin that was no longer in circulation and only worth one percent of a dollar. Still, not all individuals named Penny had her luck. Some of them flourished anyway. Maybe it was just her.

Right now, she had to focus. Get into her role. Be convincing. Be grateful for this job. Because it paid well—if she got it.

Think positive, Penny. You attract whatever you focus on. She *would* get this job. She had to. There was no turning back. No other alternative. She had ten days to do what she had to do. That was her deadline. Or she'd be dead.

Penny brushed her hair and fixed it neatly, but boringly as she got ready for her interview.

She needed this job. She was this close to getting it now. She couldn't afford to screw this up.

Excitement rushed through her. The agency said that she'd been selected but needed to pass another interview: a face-to-face match-up to see if the client and she gelled.

She had everything riding on this position. If she didn't get this full time job, she'd be gone. She owed too many people too much money. She was overdue with everything and working just to keep struggling was a pain. She was through with struggling. She needed to take whatever position she could get to survive. But this was the one she needed. She'd stalked Bianca for years. And finally she had found a way to get into her life.

Penny's life was similar to Bianca's old life. She'd read somewhere Bianca grew up not having much. Well, that was Penny's life too. Back then, she considered herself lucky to get a one meal a day and would often go hungry. When her parents died, she'd gone from foster home to foster home like an unwanted child. That's why she longed to belong somewhere.

No matter how hard she tried, she'd always get pushed back. She'd learned to make her own way. Nothing was going to stop her this time.

She'd changed up her resume to hide her past, of course. They would never suspect a thing.

Of course, the agency she was now temping for came up on top of the searches when she'd been job hunting years ago.

The Elite Executive Nanny Agency (EENA).

Earlier, Penny had re-read the company's mantra and got herself familiar with it. *We're dedicated to matching high-profile families with top nannies. Our nannies are college-educated, creative, nurturing...*

Nannies working for high profile families.

High profile families.

The words had marinated in her mind.

It was her first interview for a full time job in months. She'd been temping for months, filling in on a one-day assignment here and there, hoping for the coveted live-in nanny position for the rich. She'd joined the agency on purpose, hoping for that spot.

It wasn't her only agency. She'd been registered with several. Office temp work, nanny work, anything she could get.

This position wasn't like any other. It came with a room and board and a huge salary, working for the wealthy. And she couldn't wait to get out of her tiny shared apartment—an apartment for which she was already months behind on her share of the rent.

This job would be the solution to her financial problems.

Nannies for the super-rich could easily get a six-figure salary complete with a juicy bonus and a nice ride thrown in, not to mention their own private living quarters.

She sighed deeply.

She could really use that. But she knew she had to up her game. She'd read that these super nannies had to be good. Really good. Speak several languages, Ivy League degrees, impeccable references, presentable, fit, versed in martial arts, award-winning culinary training. They wanted the best for their little one while they traveled extensively around the globe, engaged in special high-profile events, and they required a nanny who could maintain a high level of discretion and security.

Penny would be interviewing for an A-lister couple, a rich heir and his wife who desperately needed a new nanny for their precious little three-year old to replace the previous nanny who apparently went missing without a trace.

Penny had a college degree, and thanks to her colorful employment history, she'd gained a lot of experience in different industries, including the restaurant biz, working for a security firm, subbing at a daycare, working part-time for a professional cleaning agency, among other jobs. But she also had to look the part of a super nanny.

She'd spent the last of her available credit on her card to get a mani-pedi and buy a decent suit. They wouldn't want someone looking like a scavenger anywhere near their luxury dwelling. She had to look as if she belonged in their world, not struggling to make ends meet. People who appear too desperate rarely got good breaks.

These days, you took whatever you could get. Times had changed since her parents' days when you had one job for the rest of your life and a cushy retirement from the same company. Nowadays, you'd be lucky if said company was still around with all these company mergers and closures due to the changing times. Not to mention the cost of living had skyrocketed and not kept up with salaries in most industries. No wonder she was in debt. She wasn't keeping up with the Joneses, she wasn't even keeping up with life! Food cost a fortune. Rent cost a fortune. That was why she desperately wanted a live-in position. And she'd came to the right place.

Live with the rich and get paid for it while taking care of their precious little babies. It took careful planning.

But she needed to get her money back in ten days.

Her late husband had owed some dangerous loan sharks. She had no idea until his death. She suspected they were following her. They'd made it clear they'd go after his widow if she didn't pay up by next month. She would end up like her husband—or worse. And she couldn't let that happen, especially since that criminal Bianca took everything she had.

She only had ten days to pull this off. But she had to make it look as if she would stay there longer.

Being broke didn't do much for her. Being poor affected your health, it brought on stress, and stress caused the body to get flooded with all sorts of hormones like cortisone, which accelerated the production of glucose. Chronic exposure to cortisol could increase the body's resistance to insulin. She'd learned that from her late mother, who was a Type 2 diabetic. She wanted to keep herself healthy and well, but getting stress ulcers or elevated blood pressure because of constant worrying about survival wasn't going to help much. She'd read studies about those living in poverty tended to have higher rates of health issues than wealthier people.

Food, water, shelter were the three basic needs for human survival. She'd do anything to keep surviving. She was desperate now. Desperate times called for desperate measures.

She glanced at herself in the hallway mirror. Her windowless room, which used to be a storage cupboard, barely had space for a bed. Her roommate Bex had begged her to share the apartment. Had she known it had only one legal bedroom, she would have looked away. Then again, she didn't have much choice. She'd spent the night at the homeless shelter and made her way to the employment agency the next day where they met, looking at the job board on the computer terminals.

She didn't know how her life ended up like this. With a college degree and a tight job market, even new lawyers were having a hard time finding work since everything was automated these days including apps that answered legal questions, something new lawyers used to do. She knew a few of them driving Uber now to make ends meet.

She had her degree and was about to find work as a nanny. Hell, just last week she was scrubbing toilets. But she would do what she had to do.

Bex came out of her room, hungover again. "You going out?" she said, yawning, her eyes barely open.

"I have an interview this morning."

"Got the rent?" her eyes were barely pried open.

"I told you, by the end of the month."

Money ruined friendships more than miscommunication or any other issue. Well, money and men.

Bex didn't know too much about Penny. And that was fine. She didn't know too much about her either, except that she drank too much and partied too hard and had a different guy in her room every week. Penny wasn't judgmental, but she didn't appreciate having Bex's guys hit on her, nor finding her stuff missing the next morning. The lock on the door of her tiny sleeping closet didn't work well.

It's hard to imagine they met at an employment office, of all places. Penny was staying at a shelter between 5 p.m. and 9 a.m. Residents had to be out working or looking for work between 9 and 5. Many of the residents were called the working poor. Making minimum wage but not enough to pay the rent in the city. Bex offered her room in her old rent-control unit she took over from her grandmother who'd recently passed away.

How on earth did Penny end up like this?

4. The Past

She gazed up at the sky which had now turned a deep shade of red. The color of blood, like the blood stains on her fingertips and her hands.

Her pulse pounded in her throat. She didn't have much time as she pulled up to the oak tree by the dirt road. This would be the perfect spot. No one ever came there.

Her hands were covered in blood, her shirt, her pants. She would have to change them soon, but first things first.

She turned off the headlights and shut the engine off. Moisture pooling on her face, her anxiety overruling her body. She glanced around nervously. No cars were driving by. It was an isolated area. The sound of crickets sounded in the background. Nothing else except for the heavy fast beats of her heart.

Terror.

She'd never done anything like this before. Her chest heaved. Anxiety ripped through her. It wasn't supposed to end like this. The day wasn't supposed to end like this. Why did it have to end like this? Why?

She'd never hurt a fly before, much less another human being.

She needed the money. She couldn't help it. She needed a way out.

She got out of her vehicle. Blood was everywhere. She'd have to clean the blood later—clean away all evidence.

Her breathing was labored as she popped open the trunk and saw the body in it. She gagged. She squeezed her eyes shut.

She couldn't bear to look at the lifeless body. It wasn't supposed to end like that. The blood stains on the face, the eyes, the nose, the neck.

Horror gripped her. She would never forget the face. It would haunt her forever.

She grabbed the shovel and made her way to the oak tree. She'd have to dig a grave as deep as she could to bury the body. Bury the evidence. Bury the past. Bury the pain. No one could ever know. She didn't know how she was going to keep this to herself, but she would have to. Her life depended on it. Her freedom depended on it.

She glanced around again. It was a good thing it was out there in the country, a wooded area where there were no cameras. Everyone had hidden cameras everywhere in the city. It was as ubiquitous as having a cell phone.

It took longer than she'd thought to dig into the dirt—and more laborious. She wiped the sweat off her brow. Her muscles burned. Her lungs ached. Her back was on fire.

Bury the body deep, like the memory of this event at the back of your mind.

But in her heart she knew nothing stayed buried forever. But she would deal with that later. Even if that would mean looking over her shoulder, watching her back, every moment of her life.

It was a mistake. It wasn't supposed to happen like this.

She then grabbed the stiff body, dripping with blood like her hands. Heavy as the weight of guilt on her shoulders.

She swallowed hard and placed the body in the makeshift grave, looking around, glancing nervously over her shoulders.

"Sorry," she whispered to the lifeless body. "I'm so sorry.

No one could ever know about this.

She rubbed the large cut on her forearm. That was going to leave a nasty scar.

Love of money wasn't the root of all evil, she thought to herself, *lack* of money was. Poverty was a burden and disease she did not want to have. She needed to survive.

She could try to justify it all she wanted, but deep down she knew it was wrong.

Would karma catch up with her?

She would wipe this day out of her mind forever, like the ghost of the past. *It was an accident*, she justified in her mind. *It wasn't murder. It wasn't planned.*

But hiding a body *was* a crime. At the very least, it would insinuate guilt.

Would anyone ever find out what she did? Would they understand? She had to make sure the pit was deep enough so no one would ever find the body.

If anyone found out what she did, her life would be over.

5. Penny

As Penny sat on the number 27 bus to Brock Lane Blvd, she fished inside her bag for her cell phone. Her only affordable source of entertainment these days and the safest, since she didn't have to stay out late at night. Commuting seemed to be the only time she had available to listen to an audiobook. It took her away into another world. She could tune out from everything around her while absorbing herself in another life, another story. It seemed to be the perfect escape. She had no idea how she got on without it. She was on a strict budget, so she used her library card for free audiobooks and could listen to as many as she liked. That seemed to be all she could afford right now. Everything was streamed these days.

Her commute to the other side of town, the rich area, would take about an hour in this traffic and she didn't want to be late.

Just then, a text came in from her social media account and her heart pounded hard. It read:

Password reset code: 269998

Or reset your password by clicking here:

ww.hhtp.l@kajd&#f

Yeah, right! Nice try.

She didn't even try to log in.

Hackers and scammers were everywhere. She promptly deleted it.

It was a trust-no-one society now—the verify-first-how-do-I-know-it's-not-a-scam world. She'd learned a lot from her late ex, Rexton and the crowd he hung out with. After years of unemployment, he'd resorted to all sorts of tricks to get by. He'd warned her about a lot. Sadly, like all things in life, his actions caught up with him. Still, she was glad for what he'd taught her and what she'd learned for herself.

Never. Click. Anything. Ever.

She almost fell for it once when her favorite online retailer allegedly sent her an email saying the delivery was delayed so she had to click on a link and enter in her password. Good thing she didn't, of course. And she really *had been* expecting a delivery. That's how they got people. Cast a wide net and see who took the bait.

She'd go separately to that official website and log in the usual way. Not through some scammy link where they could download malware, steal her credit card or ID, or worse.

A hacker using a bot tried to trick her social media provider, to discover or guess her password. Lesson learned, never use the word Password as your password or any crap like that. She made sure her password was something more complicated to avoid these phishing attempts.

She hated scammers.

She hated fraudsters.

She hated bullies.

She hated Bianca.

And that was why she had started to dislike Rexton. She knew she could never stay with him after he'd changed. After he'd spiralled into a dark life of deceit. But that was another matter. She would slide those memories out of her mind. She had to keep a positive aura around her now.

Your thoughts affect your behavior. They affect your mood. Your spirit. She would need to keep her spirits up to get this job.

She. Needed. This. Job.

She opened the library app on her phone and plugged in her earphones and started her audiobook. It was a love story. She enjoyed living vicariously through the characters in the story.

Speaking of characters. When she glanced up to see where the bus was going, she noticed a man dressed in blue jeans and a jacket, sitting on a seat nearby staring at her. Once she made eye contact, most people look away, but not him. Most commuters were busy, absorbed in their smartphones, staring at the screens, not other people.

Unease swept over her.

She glanced away and looked out the window, only to see that the traffic was worse than she'd expected. Looked as if there was an accident slowing the traffic.

An accident.

Her heart jumped again and squeezed in her chest. She hated accidents, and not for the obvious reasons. She always wondered because of what happened in the past, if accidents were always unintentional.

She glanced at the time on the display of her phone. It was a good thing she gave herself extra time before the interview in case of delays. She missed the days when she had enough money to grab a cab or get a ride from Rexton wherever she had to go. She wasn't a huge fan of commuting. You never know who you'd be seated beside on public transit.

From the corner of her eye, she could see that the man was still gazing in her direction. What was his problem? Her breathing quickened.

Must stay calm, Penny.

No one knows about you. It's going to be all right.

She was afraid to close her eyes, like most people who listened to audiobooks on the transit or whatever they were listening to on their smartphones. For one, she didn't want to miss her stop and two, she had to be careful about her surroundings, pick-pockets and what have you. No one wanted surprises.

She remembered hearing about one guy who'd been sleeping on a bus and was stabbed out of nowhere by some crackpot. Luckily, the creep was apprehended, as it was a crowded bus. But the victim didn't fare too well.

Stop being negative, Penny.

Sometimes, she just couldn't help it. When she was around Rexton, she became a nervous wreck. She realized now that *not* having Rexton in her life had been a blessing in disguise.

Right now, she had money on her mind. She would do anything for her money back. Money was all she could think about. She needed to get her money. It was about time. She thought about her money day and night.

6. Penny

An hour later, Penny sat in the grand dining room at the Wingarden's penthouse apartment with the panoramic view of the great lake. It was one of their many spectacular properties.

A wave of hope swept through her. She could do this. She would nail this interview and get this position. It was hers. She could feel it. The universe *had* to be good to her for once. She'd suffered enough. It was her time now.

This wasn't an ordinary job and she knew it. This was a to-die-for job. A job that paid six-figures, full benefits, involved the use of a luxury car, paid accommodation, lavish vacations and top bonuses. She wished she could keep this job for the full year, but she had to remind herself that she only had ten days to do what she had to do. Still, it would be an amazing experience if she had to resort to plan B and stay longer. It would certainly pay all her expenses and give her a year in the lap of luxury.

Focus, Penny. Focus.

Penny sat as calmly as she could at the beautiful dining table with the sunlight beaming in. If it weren't for the pristine environment, she'd swear she was in an interrogation room. She tried to pick up on the body language but it wasn't easy. Usually she could read people like a book, but not this time.

The Wingarden apartment took up the entire top floor of the building. She tried everything to keep her jaw off the floor, as if she was used to such an immaculate place. It was sheer luck that she'd done tons of volunteer work during college and ended up working for the famous Lady Eloise Dartsworth, the grand duchess who was living in North America at the time.

Lady Dartsworth had given her a top notch reference that Penny used to get listed with the nanny agency. It had only been volunteer work through college for college credits, but Lady D was nice enough not to mention that. It was an excellent reference. It opened doors for Penny. Well, sort of. Until she'd been down on her luck. But she still had that reference and the agency practically framed it on their wall.

Since then she'd done some odd babysitting errands, admin jobs, but nothing like this. No live-in positions. This was surreal.

She'd already passed the aptitude test from the agency and the reference and police check. Her CPR and First Aid were up to date. She'd taken some free refresher courses at the local college. She'd already met with Vera Wingarden who came to the agency to help screen some applicants. She wondered why her daughter-in-law and son were not there for the initial screening.

Okay, Penny. Keep calm and interview well. You need this job. You need this job, she coached herself with the powers of positive thinking she'd taken up recently. She'd read about commanding good stuff to happen for you. Operating on a positive frequency level to attract all the good things from the universe—or something like that. Back in the day, she used it write it off as psychological mumbo-jumbo crap. But right now, she was desperate.

Desperate people do desperate things.

She was sick and tired of being sick and tired—and broke and poor.

She wanted more out of life. She wanted a roof over her head, money in her hands and not always forked over to high interest credit cards that she'd used to get by.

She needed this job.

She *had* to get this job.

"No need to be nervous, Penny. Just relax. You've done very well so far," Vera said to her as if she could read her body language.

Vera concerned Penny for some strange reason. She didn't know what it was, but she didn't like it too much. But Penny had better get past it. It was as if Vera's eyes were scanning her at every turn, even when she wasn't looking directly at her. There was a strange vibe coming from her.

"I will," Penny said, sheepishly. Intimidation swept through her. She couldn't help it. The Wingardens gave off the scent of wealth and power and she must give out the scent of poverty and desperation. But she fought to get rid of it. She would cover it with a bit of confidence.

Vera peered at her over her expensive-looking wire-rimmed glasses. Her watch, her perfume, everything about her looked as if she cost more than Penny could possibly make in a lifetime.

"Now I'm Vera, as I said before. And this is my son Elvin and my daughter in-law Bianca." She pointed to the others around the table.

Penny observed the couple seated across her, each with a notepad and gold pen as if ready to jot down notes like judges in a reality show contest.

This all seemed so unreal.

Like a staged reality show. She was half-expecting to see cameras and a crew hiding somewhere.

Elvin III looked like an ordinary man, broad shoulders, well-groomed. Polite demeanor. But she'd read up on him too. He was a complete failure in his father's eyes. He worked a lot, but wasn't successful in turning the family business around in the new era.

His wife Bianca was another story altogether. Penny knew her story all too well. A con artist. A thief. A gold digger.

She thought it was odd that Bianca and Elvin were not talkative, as if this was Vera's idea and not theirs.

Penny's breath caught in her throat as she glanced at Bianca's tattoo on her forearm. It was odd that a woman like that could land an eligible billionaire from old money, given how old-fashioned they were. How one earth did Vera approve Bianca for her son?

She'd read somewhere that Bianca got pregnant soon after they met. She figured it had to be that. She had cornered him into marriage.

That witch.

Penny looked at Bianca's rose tattoo on her forearm. Her eyes drew to the image. The cut above it. So distinctive. That scar. She'd remember it anywhere, the image of the bleeding rose singed in her memory.

Penny paused, holding her breath. Waiting to see if there was any recognition from Bianca.

None.

Vacant.

Eyes used more muscles than any part of the body. Processed information around the clock for the brain.

Penny was counting on Bianca having a bit of prosopagnosia—face blindness. Penny remembered that Bianca mentioned on social media that she always forgot faces. She was at a reunion and some chick got upset because she didn't recognize her.

The average person was capable of recognizing 5,000 faces. But Bianca was exposed to many faces in her line of work with charities, social media followers and so forth so even if she was good at faces, she probably wouldn't be able to place Penny. Penny was counting on that when she applied for the job to work near Bianca.

Penny had been stalking Bianca for years now and finally got this chance to get close to her.

People divulge way too much about themselves online. It was crazy. Luckily, Bianca did it often. That's how Penny got so much information about her and kept track of what she was up to. She'd had the page long before she found her rich man to marry. Then she posted about her pregnancy test, showed off her baby bump, the engagement ring, the birth, the whole shebang.

Penny was able to snoop on her easily with the breadcrumbs of clues of her life.

Did her new family know about her real history? If they did, she'd be in a jail cell, not a palace like the one she was living in now.

Penny would get the position. She already had the interview. Just ten days. That's all she needed before they shipped the little girl off to private school. A heavily secured one at that.

Well, they were in for more trouble than they could ever possibly imagine. A scandal that would end all scandals in history.

"Nice tattoo," Penny said, noticing Bianca's eyes on her.

The tattoo was a unique three-dimensional design of a large blood-red rose that covered most of her forearm. How did the artist get the intricate design so perfect? The enormous rose looked so real. The design also included a long jagged black stem and sharp-looking prominent thorns at each side of the flower. What did that symbolize?

It was one of the most ancient symbols in the world representing suffering, sin, sorrow, and hardship. A rose was said to represent pain and pleasure. Was that what it meant for Bianca? Penny wondered. A red rose *tattoo* was also said to symbolize promise, hope and new beginnings. She'd thought of getting herself inked up once, but decided not to bother.

One could not help but staring at Bianca Wingarden's red rose tattoo. Suddenly, a pang of nausea and anxiety swept over Penny, because she knew what it really symbolized for her.

She knew more about it than anyone.

She remembered what happened the last time she'd seen a red rose tattoo.

Her whole life fell apart.

Bianca's tattoo was just so enormous and in your face. It contrasted to the demeanor of the wealthy Wingarden wife seated in the chair dressed in an elegant cream-colored sleeveless trench dress, sporting expensive diamonds on her fingers, particularly the ring finger with her gold wedding band. She oozed sophistication and money.

Money.

All that was on Penny's mind was her money. She needed her money back. Badly.

The desperation oozed from her soul, her spirit, her heart, her mind.

She needed this chance to work with the Wingardens.

She. Needed. Money. Now.

Deep breath, Penny. You'll be fine. Just focus on getting the job first. Focus on being the best nanny they could ever dream of hiring.

"Thank you," Bianca said, giving Penny an icy stare.

"Are you all right, dear?" Vera asked Penny, probably noticing the perspiration on Penny's face.

It was that red rose tattoo.

She had to shift her thoughts away from it just for once. "Yes, I'm fine, thank you." Her voice was as calm as she could make it.

She figured Vera *did* wear the pants and carry the wallet in this household. Vera was obviously the matriarch of the Wingarden dynasty and she was like a queen, in charge of the family. Vera probably had to sign off on everything and had the final say. After all, Penny would be looking after Vera's precious heiress to the Wingarden dynasty, her granddaughter. This was a critical role and Penny knew it. That was why she didn't want to screw this interview up.

But one thing Penny was taught by the agency was that job interviews were not just the opportunity for the potential employer to scrutinize candidates, it was a prime opportunity for the candidate to scrutinize the company.

It was a time to ask themselves if they really want to work for the client. It was or should be a two-way interview, but Penny already knew she wanted to work there.

They'd told her before in the first interview, they wanted the woman caring for their heir to be the best and to have the best.

She had to look as pristine as they looked. The butler had an immaculate tuxedo and was well groomed. Even the butler had a manicure; she noticed it when he opened the door to her before the interview and announced her arrival.

Everything was so orderly in the Wingarden household. They oozed wealth and power and pristine order.

Could she do this?

Could she pull this off?

What if they found about her game plan?

She was a speck of dust on their radar. She could end up in cement in the basement in one of their properties and no one would know. They had a mountain of flowing money to cover up anything and bury skeletons if they had to.

Shit.

She should go back now.

Bitch has my money. I'm not leaving without getting what's mine and messing up her life as she messed up mine.

Her mind was racing, calculating her odds, her chances, her senses.

"Now, could you please tell us about your background. About your parents? Do you have any brothers or sisters?" Vera glanced into her eyes over her glasses.

Bianca and Elvin looked at Penny attentively, waiting for her answer to Vera's question.

Elvin's arms were folded across his chest. Bianca leaned back, a smirk on her lips.

"Um..." Why did they have to ask an open question? And a question about her family? What did it matter? Penny didn't want to lie at this interview, but she didn't want to exactly tell the truth either, especially if it wasn't any of their business.

Did they think she had an ex-convict for a brother or an insane mother or drunk father? Did that matter? *Would* that matter? Her family wouldn't be doing her job, she would be. What did it matter?

Penny sighed deeply. "My parents passed away when I was young," she said, softly.

"Oh dear. I'm so sorry to hear that," Vera said. It was as if she was the only one in the room with Penny. Elvin and Bianca seemed like extras but watched her intently and took notes.

Elvin then cleared his throat as if sensing the need to say something. "Sorry to hear that. When did they pass?"

Crap.

"When I was about seven."

"Seven. Oh, that's young."

"Yes, it was. But I was raised with my grandmother. She's wonderful."

"Oh good. Where is she now?"

Penny cleared her throat. What was she going to say? "Oh, Grandma is back in Texas."

"I see."

What was this? An interview about her family?

Please. Next question. Please let it be about her job skills and what she could bring to the coveted live-in nanny position to the Wingarden household.

"Any siblings?"

She swallowed hard. She didn't have any full siblings. They were half siblings from her father's side. Okay, she'd just say no, because they were not full siblings, even though deep down Penny knew it didn't matter because family was family whether you shared two parents or not.

"No," she answered as politely as she could.

Vera continued to study Penny over her glasses rim. Penny hated that.

"Very well." Vera then wrote something on her sheet of paper and then glared back at Penny. Was she assigning a number to each question? Like a score out of ten?

"Where did you spend your early years?"

Crap. Crap. Crap.

What was she going to say? In a juvenile home? Her grandmother hadn't raised her the whole time she was a child. But she couldn't say that, could she? What was this? Twenty Questions about her personal life? What did her personal life have to do with Penny raising a child in a secured environment?

Penny had seen the security cameras earlier when she'd entered the penthouse suite. They were everywhere. In the building. In the unit. She knew she couldn't pull a fast one, so what did it matter?

She was told she'd be working at the mansion outside the city. She was willing to be that place would be even more secure. She was sure she'd have to wear a security ankle bracelet whenever she left the building or their country estate with their child in her care, especially with all the stories of nanny kidnappers and extortionists in the papers recently.

But why grill Penny about her private personal life and upbringing? It wasn't as important where you came from as to where you were now and what you planned to do with the rest of your life. She wasn't ready to share her secret past with anyone. She didn't know if she'd ever be ready. Her past was dead and gone and that's where she'd leave it. In the past. "I spent my early years in Texas with my maternal grandmother. She was wonderful. We used to go to church on Sundays and she always raised me to do the right thing."

That wasn't *completely* a lie.

She noticed the smile of approval on Vera's lips. That had to be a good thing, right?

"Good. Your grandmother seems like a wonderful person," Vera said. She marked a score out of ten on her sheet.

Was she seriously grading Penny in this interview? Was she going to do this with all their applicants? Penny had heard from the agency that she'd been narrowed down to three top candidates. She wondered if the other two had interviewed yet.

She wondered just how many candidates they interviewed for this position. Then again, if she were in their position, she'd be careful who she hired to live in her home and care for her child, too.

Bianca didn't seem to care either way. Was this the way she was with her child?

"Okay, now what are your hobbies and interests?"

Why did that matter?

"Well, I love to act."

Vera frowned. "Act?"

"Yes, I studied to be an actress back in..." Penny's voice trailed off. Vera didn't look too pleased that she had an interest in theatre.

"That sounds interesting," Bianca finally spoke, her lips curved slightly, but the smile didn't touch her eyes. They were cold and calculating and penetrated Penny.

"Yes, my grandmother had encouraged me to be in the Christmas play at the church and..."

"Oh, that sounds grand," Vera added.

"Yes, it was a grand experience," Penny tried to match Vera's vocabulary.

She desperately needed this job, maybe she would act the part they wanted.

Wasn't life an act anyway? We were all giving a performance everyday whether we realized it or not. Someone once said life was like a novel filled with suspense. Each page told a different story, a different experience. Life was an adventure to be enjoyed, right until the last page.

"What would you say are your greatest strengths?" Vera continued.

Wasn't Bianca or Elvin going to ask Penny any questions since it was their child? Didn't they care? Or did they just leave all the worrying to the Vera, the head of the Wingarden dynasty since Elvin II passed away?

"I care deeply."

"Oh?"

"Yes. Sometimes too much. I love working with children and I care deeply about their wellbeing. I think children should be given as much love and devotion and attention. They should be nurtured to grow to their fullest potential. Laughter should always be a part of their day," Penny rambled on with lines from one of her plays.

But she meant it. She'd always chosen her roles carefully at the theatre workshops at the prison.

7. Penny

"So why did you decide to become a nanny?" Vera asked, pointedly. "Wouldn't you prefer acting?"

This was a trick question, wasn't it?

"Well, I love acting. I studied it in high school. I took drama electives. I think the role of drama therapy with children is so important. I wanted to combine it with my work with children. Children should be able to express themselves in a healthy environment and pretend play is a healthy part of child development, using the imagination and so on."

Vera looked pleased with the answer. The more Penny got into the role, she more she felt comfortable. She could do this. She could win them over.

She *must* get this role. She must get this *position*, she corrected herself in her mind.

Vera then gave a mark out of ten for Penny's answers, while both Bianca and Elvin looked on nodding politely, pretending to take notes, but Penny looked across the table and by chance, she saw Bianca doodling something on the sheet of paper. It looked like notes on errands she had to do. She hoped the errands were related to her child. Shouldn't she be all one hundred percent invested in this interview as her mother in-law was?

What was going on with this family? Strange people indeed.

She couldn't wait to get her money and get out of there.

Be positive, Penny. Stop looking at negative things. Nothing is perfect. You need this job. You need a roof over your head. You need a regular pay check.

Penny tried to sweep the negative talk out of her mind and refill with positive affirmations. She'd read while at the prison that if you feed yourself negativity, you'll live and breathe negativity. If you feed yourself positivity, you'll live and breathe positivity. She wanted to experience a positive flow in her life for a change.

Yes, change. This was about a new change.

"What qualities do you have that make you a good caregiver?"

Penny thought for a moment. She had to be careful, very careful how she answered each question. Her *life* depended on it.

"I love children. And I love working with children. I believe having a high level of enthusiasm for this job is crucial as it isn't always easy. I pay close attention to details. I notice things a lot. And that's important because safety is always important with little ones especially at that age. Three," she added. She knew she'd be caring for their three-year-old daughter *if* she got the job.

"Good," Vera said, a smile curving the corner of her lips.

Penny peered over at Elvin who seemed very kind in his expression. Then she looked at Bianca. She'd given her a stony glare, as if to see if Penny would be competition. But wasn't she chosen because she seemed like the least likely threat of all the other candidates? Penny had taken great care with her appearance this morning. Simple. Clean, yet homely. She didn't wear her wired cup push-up bra so that her chest would seem more flat. And she dressed as Victorian as she could in the modern era with a shirt buttoned all the way up to her neck.

God, she couldn't wait to get out of this disgusting blouse. The collar felt like a noose around her neck. But there was no way she was showing any kind of cleavage or worldly vibe. Her skirt went all the way down to her ankles and her hair was brushed very neatly into a bun. Come to think of it, that's probably why that guy on the bus was staring her down earlier. She looked like a freak in the modern world.

A feeling of encouragement flooded Penny's soul. She was on a roll now. She was *in* a role now. And she would perform it the best she could to win the coveted reward. The chance to have a good roof over her head and a dream job—and her money back from that con artist Bianca.

"Childhood should be about fun," Penny continued, "Children shouldn't have to worry about anything. My role would be to ensure that you can go about your day-to-day activities," she said, addressing Elvin and Bianca, "without worrying about your child. I'll keep her entertained, nourished, and ensure she has all that she needs. I'm also a compulsive cleaner," she added for good measure. "I love to clean, so while the children are relaxing, I'm happy to do light housework."

Vera scribbled some notes with enthusiasm on her notepad while Bianca looked on with what looked like an air of suspicion. Was Penny trying too hard? Would Bianca suspect she had ulterior motives?

Shit.

Did Bianca recognize her?

She adjusted her glasses on her nose. Penny didn't usually wear glasses, but she picked up a cheap pair from the drug store to make sure she looked different.

"Have we met before?" Bianca asked, narrowing her eyes.

Penny's heart raced. The heavy pounding of her heart in her chest smashed against her rib cage. Sweat moistened her hairline. "Um...I...I don't think so," she said, softly, pushing her glasses up on her nose as they slid down slightly due to the sweat on her face.

Was she busted? Did Bianca recognize her?

"Never mind," Bianca said. "I thought you look familiar."

Vera cleared her throat.

Elvin gave his wife an unusual look, then went back to his notes.

Poor unsuspecting Elvin. He had no idea whom he was married to. The woman who trapped him with a pregnancy to get his money. That's what Bianca was all about. Money. And she would do anything to get it.

Well, Bianca had Penny's money and she was going to give her money back to her—and go to prison, if Penny could help it.

"And is there anything else we should know about you, Penny?" Vera asked, eagerly.

"Oh, yes. I'm punctual."

"Yes, you are." Vera glanced at her expensive-looking designer gold watch. Penny couldn't tell the make, but based on the sparkling diamond crusts lining the front, she was willing to bet that watch cost more than she would be making in the entire year.

"I notice you were twenty minutes early, unlike our last interviewee," Vera added.

Well, that was encouraging.

"I also notice your nails are clean and cut short, but a professional manicure would be better next time," Vera added.

"Oh?" *I* had *a professional manicure. A cheap one, but still professional.*

"Yes, we look at things like grooming, dear. If you're to take care of children, you need to know how to take good care of yourself," Vera said with a slight curl of her lips. She then scribbled a score out of ten on her sheet of paper.

Penny felt as if she was being graded all over again, just like in high school. If she didn't know Vera was one of the wealthiest housewives in America, she'd swear she was a strict schoolteacher by trade.

"Are you flexible with your schedule?" Vera asked again.

"Oh, yes, ma'am. I'm very flexible." *Because I have no other life outside of a job right now.*

"Do you have other commitments?" Vera asked the question, but Penny thought it was sneaky. She knew what Vera meant by her question. She meant did Penny have any significant others that might interfere with her ability to be on-call twenty-four seven. They were looking for simple, homely spinsters for this position, weren't they? They probably didn't want anyone bringing in shady characters around their child or grandchild. Well, that was all right, because Penny wanted this position and so she could fit herself into the role.

Besides, Rexton was dead now.

"Not really. Not at the moment."

"Good." Bianca seemed relieved.

Elvin gave Bianca a stare. The chemistry between them was unusual, Penny noticed. It seemed as if he gave her signals on behaving herself, but half the time, she seemed to ignore it.

"What happened to your last job?" Vera asked.

"My last job?" Penny swallowed hard, hoping they wouldn't notice. Penny repeated the question deliberately, stalling for time to make something up that sounded acceptable.

It had been so long since she worked for the grand duchess. What could she possibly say she was doing in the meanwhile?

"Well, I've been with the agency," Penny finally said. And her statement wasn't untrue. though she worked in an admin capacity until something suitable came up. "I've been doing various short-term assignments while I got settled here in the city."

"Oh, yes."

"Yes, Ma'am."

Well, to be truthful, she'd gotten settled into a homeless shelter run by a mission in the Lower East side of town, but she wasn't about to go into details about that. She only hoped they didn't probe too much. She'd told them before that she was staying with a cousin. She was sure she wouldn't get the job working for the super-rich if she'd been sleeping in a homeless shelter.

"What do you enjoy about taking care of children?"

Don't say everything. Don't say everything.

"I love their laughter, their energy, their spirit. It is wonderful being around children. It makes me feel connected to my own childhood. As clichéd as this sounds, children are the future and it's important that we nurture them to grow up to their full potential." And she really meant that.

Besides, with all the bad news happening in the world today and the stories dominating the headlines of gloom and doom, she loved being around children who didn't have a clue about all the grown-up stuff. When children grew into adults, sometimes they forgot to laugh, to enjoy life to the fullest, to shrug off negative stuff and focus on what made them happy. She loved the way they were. That was how everyone should be. They should never forget the child in them. They should never forget to have fun—to laugh.

Little Evie sounded like a joy to take care of. She wanted this job more than anything in more ways than one.

"What kinds of activities would you do with Evie?" Vera asked, leaning forward.

"Well, I would dress very casually in jeans and apron and be prepared to get down and have tons of messy fun that we'd clean up afterwards. At that age, three, children are exploring, they love fun and colors and Playdough. I'd also fill up a table with books and we'd do tons of reading."

Vera lit up. Her eyes widened in appreciation. Bianca narrowed her eyes more intently in Penny's direction. Elvin tried to warm her up by rubbing her shoulders, getting her to loosen up a bit.

Penny could tell Vera was a bookish person. Most wealthy women that age had a taste for fine literature and Penny knew all too well the importance of literacy.

Score.

"We'd also doodle with markers on cardboard. Play doctor with dolls. Take a walk around the home and hunt for colors.

We'd play with puzzles, look at family photos together, create with peel and stick jewel. That sort of thing."

"We live in a house outside the city. You would be spending the majority of your time there

She almost forgot they had several residences. Shit, the house they spoke about was comparable to a royal palace. She'd seen many images of it online.

Vera looked pleased.

Penny could feel her energy of acceptance from across the table. There was one thing about Penny was that she knew how to prepare for a role. She'd rehearsed this a million times. But she also meant every word of it. She desired to give the child in her care every bit of love and nurturing that she'd missed out on when she was a child.

"Are you interested in occasionally caring for other children while my grandchild has a friend over for a play date?"

"Oh, absolutely." As long as they were just as well-behaved, of course. But then again, if they weren't, what could she do about it? Penny reminded herself that she had to be Mary Poppins and would do anything to be the best live-in nanny ever.

Even if she'd only be there for a short time.

At first, she was overwhelmed with these questions, but soon realized that she'd be living in their dwelling, taking care of their child, so it was necessary for them to scrutinize every part of her life and ask questions to ensure she knew what she was doing. It wasn't everyone who was cut out to work with children. She knew that all too well. She'd had the worst caregivers growing up, going from group home to group home. Not everyone was the same, or gave the same level of care. But

Penny was going to be different. She would put a thousand percent into her job. She wanted to be the best nanny Evie could ever have.

Even if it was for a short time.

She answered questions on her ability to handle a medical emergency. And of course, that included calling 9-1-1. But she also was fully trained in First Aid and CPR and had her certificates up to date. She'd answered their questions on what she would do in a case of a child getting a blow to the head or choking or having a high fever. Again, she answered with confidence and she seemed to win over the heart and trust of the true leader of the household, Mrs. Vera Wingarden.

After about an hour and a half of grilling, the interview was finally coming to an end. The agency had warned her that the Wingardens were particular and the interview would be long. Well, she knew they were probably testing her personality to see if she had patience or if she'd start to get restless with too many questions.

Good way to screen people.

She knew that most interviews were also a behavioral analysis more than anything else.

Vera turned to her son and daughter in law. "Do you two have any other questions?"

Any other questions? They barely asked *any* questions to begin with. Vera was the one doing all the talking.

"No. You've asked everything important," Bianca said and placed her pencil down. For a mother, she sure was passive about this.

But then again, she only got pregnant for Elvin to get to his money. So why should she care about the kid? She gave him an heir. She got her life of luxury.

"Okay," Vera said, scribbling down some notes on her pad. "We've made a decision." Her smile was bright and wide.

"Oh," Penny said, joy flooding over her. She knew that when they made a decision on the spot that it could mean one thing. She got the position.

"I'm afraid you're not the candidate we're looking for."

Penny felt her stomach sink. "Oh?"

Her heart stopped beating. But... How could she have read them so wrong? Was it something she said? "Oh, I'm so sorry about that. I was really hoping to be the best nanny for your child...and your grandchild. Well, thank you for your time," Penny said, as bravely as she could.

"Thank you for *your* time, Penny," Vera said as she got up from the table.

All three of them rose, as did Penny.

This was her cue.

She flunked the interview for the dream job of her life. Did they know about her background? Were they just pretending? Were they hoping she'd reveal that she lived at the Mission homeless shelter months ago and was now sharing a tiny apartment with an addict and was behind on her share of the rent?

It was over. She had no job. No place to sleep. No money in the bank. Nothing.

Now what was she going to do?

8. Penny

Penny's spirit was deflated. She *didn't* get the job? How could she not? They seemed to be so into her? Or had she read them wrong?

Where did I go wrong?

What did I say that was so off?

She thought she performed well for the position, the interview, but it was clear that she overestimated her talent for winning approval from people. Maybe she should go back and re-read *How to Win Friends and Influence People*, because *clearly* she did something wrong.

She swung her bag around her left shoulder and smiled politely as she walked out of the grand dining room overlooking a breathtaking view of the waterfront, and into the foyer with its shiny marble cream and gold flooring. It must have cost a fortune to decorate this suite. The immaculate art work on the wall made it look like a museum. She couldn't imagine a child living there.

Penny felt her heart squeeze in her chest. She so wanted this job. She really thought she had this job in the palm of her hand.

She continued to walk with her head held high and a pleasant expression on her face, even though she was dying inside.

The place was a dream. It seemed more like a palace in the sky than a penthouse condominium suite. She had her heart set on working there and living there and at their other dwelling, the mansion, but now it would all be a faded memory.

How was she going to get her money back from Bianca, the con artist, now?

She refused to give in to her sinking feelings.

You can't control what happens to you, you can only control your reaction to it. Your response.

She remembered her therapist telling her that one day. We could not control what happened to us, only what happens within us. Happiness was not about your position in life but your *disposition*. She remembered to not blame others for your problems. Maybe she didn't ace it as she thought.

It's going to be all right, Penny. It has to be all right. Just keep believing that. Keep giving out that vibe.

She felt sick. She felt bile rise up in her. She felt as if she was going to vomit all over the elegant décor of the place.

Don't do it, girl. Deep breath. It's not the end of the world.

So they didn't give her the job she was dying to get. So what? Life went on. She'd survive somehow. She just had to. Her mind was the only thing she had to keep going right now. So what if she lost this job? She wasn't going to lose her mind over it. Once you lose your mind, that's it. She was going to hold tight to her sanity. Her hope. Whatever that meant, where ever that led her.

"Sorry again," Vera said, confidently.

Did she really mean it?

Penny was tempted again to ask her how she managed to make such a rash decision without comparing her to the other candidates. Didn't they still have one more to interview? Did she suck *that* bad? Were their enthusiastic reactions all in Penny's mind?

"No worries. I was hoping to be Evie's super fun nanny, but whoever you choose to go with, I hope she's happy with her."

Penny would be as gracious as those actors who lost out in the best supporting actor category at the Oscars. She would genuinely cheer on whoever won, even though deep down she wanted to win the award.

Later, after the butler opened the glass French doors leading to another section and she slipped her shoes back on, she gave them a polite and appreciative smile. "Thanks again."

"No, thank *you* for coming." Vera's hands were clasped together in front of her.

She'd read somewhere that the penthouse suite cost around $100 million. Imagine that. Just for an apartment. Thought it wasn't just any apartment.

The steel-shiny gold-plated elevator doors that opened up into the suite slid open for Penny and she walked inside, thanking them again and holding on tightly to her bag, as if that would stop her from fainting.

She kept playing over the interview in her mind, over and over again. Where had she gone wrong? What had she said that turned them off? Maybe it was nothing she said. Maybe they just didn't like her for whatever reason. That was the thing about working for other people. It sucked royally if they didn't take to you for whatever reason. She'd always dreamed of working for herself one day, perhaps opening up a drama school for kids or her own daycare. At least she'd be her own boss. The focus would be on her business, not her.

When she got down to the lower level of the building, the doors slid open again.

"How did the interview go?" The doorman asked her politely.

She had told him earlier she was there for an interview for a nanny job for the Wingardens. He'd wished her good luck. That was so sweet of him. People were so kind in that neighbourhood. The doorman, the service people, the affluent. They all seemed to take the time to be polite. Or perhaps they were performing too. It was easy to be happy when you had no money problems. She wasn't naïve about money though. She knew very well that money couldn't buy happiness, but it sure could rent it for a moment.

"I didn't get the job," she said with a soft pouty expression. "But I hope they're happy with whoever they chose. They're such nice people."

Always say kind things about people behind their back. Always think positive things about others, what you give out, you receive, her grandma had once told her. That was before she was too ill to care for her and before Penny had to go to foster care.

"Aww. Sorry to hear you didn't get the job. Hope you have better luck in your next interview."

Next interview?

She didn't know if she had the strength to go through that again right now. Rejection really did a number to her nerves and her self-esteem. She had to go into repair before she could muster up the courage to go through that again. Giving her best performance only to be told she just didn't cut it.

"Thank you," she said softly.

"Can I get you a cab?"

She didn't want it to look so bad that she couldn't possibly afford a taxi fare right now.

"Thank you, but I'll be fine. Just going for a quick walk in the park."

He nodded politely. "Have a good day, Ma'am."

"Thank you," she said, glancing at his name tag. "Charles."

He smiled. "You're welcome, Ma'am. Not many people take the time to call me by name."

She smiled and was on her way down the street. The brisk wind blowing her dark tendrils into her face. She let the breeze cool her skin and enjoyed the feel of fresh air. She needed air right now. She needed to think.

What would be her next strategy? How was she even going to get her money back now from Bianca the con artist? What was she going to do now?

She was so sure she'd get the position. The agency had told her she was the most qualified for the position.

When she arrived at the park, she walked through to find an empty park bench. She sat down and took out her cell phone.

She made a mistake. She didn't have a plan B for what she'd do if she didn't get the job. That was because she was determined to get it. She silently prayed to the universe to cut her a break, to make this happen. If one door closed, another would open. That's what she believed. That's what she hoped.

She saw a hotdog stand nearby and the grumbling in her stomach told her she needed to eat something or she'd pass out in the middle of the park, which would not be a good thing. She was Penny of no fixed address. Her roommate Bex had already told her she'd have to go if she didn't pay up this week.

Tears misted her eyes. She needed to take care of herself. She only had one body, just like everyone else.

When Penny turned around and went back to her seat with her hotdog, she thought she saw a man pretending to read a newspaper and glance up at her. Was it her imagination?

It had to be. She was clean. She hadn't broken any laws. She was just sitting in the park having a hotdog.

He kept looking at her. Yes, he was looking directly at her.

Then, he folded up his newspaper and got up and walked away, glancing over his shoulders. Most people read on their mobile devices these days, but she guessed this older gentleman liked the old-school ways.

She sighed deeply and took another bite, tasting the tangy sausage and the ketchup and onions she'd thrown on.

Just then she glanced down at her phone as it vibrated.

She'd forgotten that she'd turned off the ringer in case someone called her while she was in the interview. Not that many people called her, of course. But just in case.

She was stunned to see the name on the display:

E. WINGARDEN

Did she leave something behind at the apartment? Curiosity got the best of her, but right now she was too pissed to answer the phone. They'd made their premature decision and told her she was no good for the job. Why on earth were they calling her now?

It stopped ringing.

Then it rang again.

This time it was a call with a different name on the display.

V. WINGARDEN

What was going on? The Wingardens were strange folks. They'd pretty much told her she was not good enough with a don't-call-us-we'll-call-you kind of vibe. Penny just didn't get it.

She sighed deeply. Maybe she *did* leave something behind.

Okay, fine, she would see what they wanted. She answered the call. "Hello," she answered cautiously, thinking maybe they'd dialled her by mistake.

There was no sound on the other end of the phone line.

9. Penny

"Hello?" Penny asked again, her heart pounding in her chest.

Was this some sort of sick game? What was wrong with these creepy rich folks?

"Hello," the voice sounded finally. "Is this Penny?"

"Yes. Hi, Mrs. Wingarden?"

"Hi. Penny could you please return to the condo? You left something behind."

"I did?"

"Yes. I will be here for the next fifteen minutes."

"Oh, um...Okay."

"Great."

She heard a click as the call ended. How strange was that?

Penny searched through her bag. What on earth had she left behind?

Was this some sort of joke?

Shit.

She remembered she'd printed off some information from Bianca's social media page. Pictures of her and popular posts. Shit. Shit. Shit.

She couldn't find it in her bag. Had she pulled it out by mistake and dropped it on their floor or in the building? Penny had looked online at the library to go through all of Bianca's social media feeds. As much as possible given her timeframe. Something just didn't make any sense. Bianca took a lot of pictures and in some of them she did not cover her scar. She got the scar *after* she met him. But she go got the tattoo before then. She'd even printed off a copy of the tattoo to make sure she could do a positive match to be a thousand per cent sure it was really her.

Ten minutes later, Penny was back at the Wingarden's luxury condo apartment, but it was a different doorman than Charles. This man was not as friendly.

"Yes, Ma'am?"

"Hi, I have an....I mean I had an interview with the Wingardens earlier. They called and told me I left something behind. My name is Penny."

He did not say anything but reached into his pocket and pulled out his cell phone. He then moved away and proceeded to talk into the phone. "Yes, Ma'am. She's here." His voice was low but she could still hear what he was saying.

Penny was tempted to roll her eyes, but she did not. Something was a bit off. But there were cameras everywhere. They wouldn't do anything dodgy would they? They couldn't. They wouldn't get away with it.

Stop being paranoid, Penny. These are nice people. It's an upscale environment. No need to worry.

Unlike the other doorman, this one didn't wear a name tag. "You may go up to the suite, Ma'am," he said, calmly as he led her to the private elevator and gave her access. The doors then slid open and she went inside. He entered a code and she was up again toward the luxury suite in the sky with the odd wealthy family.

When the doors slid open to the Wingarden suite, the doorman Charles was there, to Penny's surprise. He gave her a polite nod and went into the elevator after she stepped off.

What was going on?

"Hi," Penny said politely, walking into the suite. "You said I left something behind?"

"Yes, dear. Thank you so much for coming back. You left your job."

"My *what*?"

Was this woman deranged?

Penny glanced around looking for hidden cameras. Maybe she was on some sort of strange reality show.

"You have the job," Vera said.

"But I thought...."

"Oh, no dear. We wanted to see how an applicant handled disappointment. We told each of you that you didn't get the position. And you were the only candidate who was positive about it. You remained in good spirits and that's what's important. Charles told us how polite you were to him and how you responded after your disappointment. We judge people by how they treat others in different positions. It's all right to smile and be polite to those who you believe have wealth and power, but what about others? You were kind to the help. And it's easy to treat people well when everything goes your way, but what about when it doesn't? We don't just want anyone working with our little Evie. And furthermore, we need to do this to make sure we have people who are more than just good on paper. We like to test their *character*."

Holy shit!

These people were not for real, were they?

"Anyone can be joyful when they get what they want," Vera continued, as Penny's jaw remained open, "but how do you handle not getting what you want in life?"

"Wow. I...um...I don't know what to say."

"You're the type of person we want around our child. My grandchild," she corrected. Congratulations, dear. The job is yours."

Penny was speechless. Her heart sank. If only they knew. So the interview was a game, was it?

She didn't know how she felt about them toying with her emotions like that, making her feel as if she'd gotten a position and pulled the rug on her to see how she would react. She wasn't a lab rat for crying out loud.

Deep breath, Penny.

Breathe in two-three, and out two-three.

Well, okay, she did see their point, but damn. She guessed, the other gal didn't take it too well, thinking she was getting the job.

Okay, life was a game, wasn't it? So Penny would just have to play her part really well.

10. Penny

Three days later, on Monday, Penny was picked up in a limousine and taken to the grand Wingarden estate in Sun Valley, Ontario, a two-hour drive north of Toronto.

The limo pulled through the gold-accented iron gates after security let them in. They drove up a long stone-path driveway to the main mansion with a stone statue and waterfall out front. It was breathtaking. She could not believe she would be living there for the duration of her contract. Though it seemed far from civilisation, she was told she would have access to her own car to take Evie to outings approved by Vera.

The butler had ushered them in through the main French doors. The place looked more like an art gallery or museum with its marble floors and gold fixtures, cathedral ceiling with a crystal chandelier. The marble stone stairways winding led up to the second floor.

Her jaw dropped. She had to remember to keep her mouth shut and not drool. She was afraid to touch anything.

It was hard to believe a three-year old roamed the halls there. It was hard to imagine a child lived there.

The Wingardens had three main residences, not counting their villas in Spain, France and Italy and their vacation homes in Florida. She had read up on the many homes they owned. Unlike the condo on the lake in downtown Toronto where she'd interviewed last week on Friday, this home, the Wingarden Mansion, was their main estate built in the early 1900s. A massive palace-like structure that had many roads going to it including a 16-car garage on Wingarden Boulevard right beside the home.

Penny would need a tour of the premises and a map of where everything was located.

Sweet. She would need a map for what she was about to do. She needed to know where her exits were. Where all the potential little secret hiding places could be.

She was stunned at all the luxuries little Evie had. They'd even named a tiny private road Evie Wingarden Blvd after their daughter Evie, after getting approval from the city of Sun Valley, so that she could boast to her friends that was *her* street. Evie Wingarden Blvd held a life-size dollhouse, the largest play house in the world according to some record sites, carefully decorated with bright colors and all the fanciest artwork and tricked out with toys for a little girl. It was called Evie's Dollhouse according to the name on the pink letter box outside.

The house was listed as Number One, Evie Wingarden Blvd, and was big enough for adults to fit inside. It looked like a classy miniature cottage complete with veranda and surrounded by white picket fences. It was surrounded by trees and she even had a treehouse to go along with it and a make-believe pool area, with no water in it for safety reasons.

Her mother, Bianca, had commissioned it and, of course, it ended up on her social media page and garnered 1.2 million likes and 150,000 shares. Because that's what life was about for Bianca. It wasn't enough to have money, she had to show it off in every way possible. One had to out-do every other social media influencer out there. Penny felt as if Bianca just used her daughter as a prop to show off in public, then dumped her in a toy box when she was done showing her off for tons of likes.

Penny also received a tour of Evie's bedroom which was fit for a princess. She glanced at all the photos. There was a baby photo of her with her parents while they were at the hospital right after her birth. Penny remembered seeing that on the social media feed. That image got hundreds of thousands of likes.

Evie must have been a few hours old in the picture. She still had the hospital sheets around her.

Bianca looked stressed and tired in that photo and that red-rose tattoo was so in your face. Penny loathed it. She knew what it really symbolized. Her heart galloped when she saw it.

The red rose. The blood-red rose tattoo.

Still, the kid did not lack for anything. She had it all. Whatever she needed, she got. She had a feeling Vera was behind all of this. After all, it looked as if Vera held the keys to the bank vault.

On some gossip sites, there were rumors about Elvin II not trusting his own son or wife and vowing to leave everything to charity if he did not have a grandchild.

Elvin III produced a grandchild before his death, so now everything could very well be in the child's name to be held in trust until she turned 18.

Of course, the family were free to help themselves to a portion of it to maintain their lifestyle which would benefit the granddaughter, of course.

Those were rumors, of course. She had to find out what was true and what wasn't. And just how much money these folks really had access to. Either way, Bianca had Penny's money. And she needed to give her money back.

Period.

They must have some liquid assets.

They could even sell off one of their properties for cold, hard cash.

Evie's great-grandfather, the great Elvin Wingarden the first, had built that mansion and half the town. A Wingarden Department Store wasn't far from there.

But that was probably why they were rumored to be having financial troubles. Didn't people realize that all these fancy amusement parks and massive estates were wonderful, but they cost a shit ton of bucks to maintain, like millions of dollars a year? How could one afford that for generations to come?

Money wasn't exactly an infinite resource, at least not anymore in this fast-paced, ever-changing world where industries could vanish overnight with a sudden turn in trends and markets.

"This will be your living quarters," Vera said to Penny as she guided her through the hallway to a suite. The walls were adorned with oil paintings from previous generations of Wingardens. She'd already received the grand tour of the east wing where they would spend most of their time. Each wing had its own rooms. She'd seen the east wing study, the living room, grand kitchen, art room, dining room, ball room and theatre room as well as the library and the play room. One of the play rooms. The west wing had similar suites but was mostly for business purposes. Vera had also given her a tour of her executive suites where her office was located.

Bianca and Elvin III stayed mostly in the north wing and the west wing.

Moments before, Vera had summoned her secretary to bring the contract to Penny's quarters for Penny to sign. She wondered why they didn't sign it in the grand dining area at the condo.

Penny glanced around the enormous room. She could not believe this would be her living quarters. It was immaculate. A dream job indeed. And just to think, this would be her dwelling for as long as she was part of the Wingarden household. They considered her family now. She'd never known what it was like to have a real family of her own, after her parents died.

"Is everything to your liking, Penny?" Vera asked her.

"Oh, yes, Ma'am."

"Very good."

The room looked as if it was a page out of one of those glossy interior decorating magazines she'd flip through while in the checkout line at the supermarket, when she couldn't even afford the price of the magazine.

Her room was beside Evie's room, which was convenient.

She looked at the windows. Was the mesh screen behind the glass easy to open if she needed an escape? She would have to figure that out later.

Penny had her cell phone with her so she could take snapshots and record any conversation that could incriminate Bianca. She had it all planned out. She was going to get Bianca to confess to her crime and give her money back to her.

The nanny suite featured a luxury designer bed with custom handmade African walnut bedframe which cost over

$200,000, from what she remembered seeing on Bianca's social media feed, and it had an iPad holder, swivel flat screen television, gold and stainless steel work and hidden compartments for her to store her things.

Holy crap! They were allowing the nanny to sleep on that bed?

Of course it was nothing compared to the master suite. Bianca had featured her bedroom on her social media account and showed off her Italian-designed supreme bed that cost an unbelievable $6.3 million. Yes, Bianca Thomas Wingarden splurged over six million dollars on a bed!

She wondered how her mother-in-law felt about that.

That kind of cash could feed a nation. It could give a million families a place to lay their head. This was insane!

The Italian-designed supreme bed was hand carved with an interior composed of 24 carat gold that weighed over 200 lbs. The exterior was lacquered and decorated with 107 kg of 24k gold. The bed also featured the finest Italian silk and cotton.

She could not believe she was really there. Up close and personal. For now.

"Don't be so surprised dear," Vera said with a smile as she carefully watched Penny's expression. "You will be doing a lot of work, so you must have peaceful sleep. We spend a quarter of our lives in bed, recharging, replenishing our souls and bodies and our brains. Sleeping quarters are very important. The more luxurious and restful and peaceful your sleep is, the better you are able to function."

That was so thoughtful of Vera.

Guilt tore at Penny's insides. She wasn't planning to stay long. Just ten days and she would be, *should* be out of there. Hopefully, alive.

Focus, Penny. Focus. Bianca is a monster. She has your money. And that's the least of what she did. They need to know about her. She should be put away for what she did.

Penny felt sore that she was about to expose the Wingardens' pristine orderly life and turn it upside down. How would they feel about her soon? This was calm and serene. The calm before the scandalous storm that was about to be unleashed.

"Well. I...thank you."

This was more than she'd expected. She knew she would have to earn her keep, her pay and her stay and she would. She felt bad for what she was planning on doing if her plans did not come to fruition. But she reminded herself: she needed her money back. Principles were principles. And Bianca was a big con artist. The worst kind. If only her husband knew.

Yes, she had it all planned out. Now all Penny had to do was pretend to be the doting nanny. It had been a good move to dress simply compared to the supermodel nannies. She was seen as less of a threat. But oh, would they be surprised in ten days. She would be their biggest threat. She was going to have to bring down the Wingardens. Well, Bianca Wingarden. The monster of the mansion.

She was glad Bianca didn't recognize her face. That was the thing with narcissistic people: they didn't pay any attention to other people.

Getting the job meant getting close to the famous Bianca with the twenty million followers and hundreds of thousands of likes and sponsorships.

Penny only had fifteen followers. She didn't care. Quality over quantity. Likes and followers did not determine your worth.

They discussed Penny's tasks and her to-do lists and to listen out for when Evie woke up and to tend to her every need. Luckily, they had a cook to carefully prepare gourmet meals including a breakfast that included fresh organic fruit picked from the garden, tossed whipped cream pancakes and fluffy scrambled eggs or a hard-boiled egg decorated with Evie's favorite Disney characters. Each meal had to be decorated. Thank goodness that wasn't Penny's job. They had someone do everything for Evie, including her own stylist who did her hair.

Why on earth would they need a nanny? Penny wondered. The mother didn't have to lift a finger or even talk to Evie!

It was insane. She'd met Evie's staff. This three-year old had her own *staff*! Penny was just Evie's personal aide or help, if she needed anything or whenever the parents were on vacation or at gala events and needed someone to watch their daughter or deal with her tantrums.

"We want our nanny to be well-rested to do her job," Vera continued.

Penny arched a brow. She could not. Believe. This.

11. Penny

After Penny signed the non-disclosure agreement, she received her contract along with tons of paperwork. She felt as if she were back in college again.

The non-disclosure agreement would prevent her from releasing secret information to outside parties. She memorized the part that read that if the party violated the non-disclosure agreement, they could be liable for damages. She also had to sign a non-compete agreement which was odd. She supposed they didn't want her working as a nanny for anyone else.

She went over the five-page nanny agreement which was daunting. She had to be careful what she signed. She didn't know why, but she just didn't trust them too much. Especially the red rose tattooed Bianca.

Dear Penny Andirs,

Welcome to the Wingarden family!

The following contract is to make sure we are all on the same page about duties, expectations, hours to be worked, vacation days, payments and other matters.

The attached "Nanny Rules" and "Daily Schedule" will help you to understand how things work at the Wingarden Mansion and should help you better understand our routines.

She glanced at the section that read compensation and she was gobsmacked. She knew it would be a six-figure salary but to see the numbers on the page, made her heart giddy.

Compensation is $130,000 per annum, paid monthly

Vehicle: Provided by the Wingardens. Employee will maintain a mileage log and submit to employer for reimbursement at the end of the pay period.

Parking: Paid for by the Wingardens

Benefits: Full health, dental, medical,

Bonus: Annual bonus minimum: $10,000 per year.

Holy shit! There were years when she didn't even make that "bonus" amount while working her butt off at two low-paying part time jobs! Her nerves got the best of her. They were so generous. How could she want to take their money? But it was her money. She needed her money back.

College tuition at $10,500 per year.

Mobile phone service at $450 per month

Employee will receive the following paid time off: family sick leave, appointments...

Employer will require 2 weeks' notice for vacation time or appointments unless emergency appointments.

Penny loved the paid holiday segment:

Employer will provide the following paid Holidays (check any that apply): All statutory holidays including Canada Day, Good Friday and Easter Monday, Christmas Day and Boxing Day, Labour Day...

She read the confidentiality agreement:

Employee understands that any and all private information obtained about the employers or their dependents during the course of employment, including but not limited to medical, financial, legal, and career, are strictly confidential and may not be disclosed to any third party for any reason.

Her eyes drifted to the grounds for termination section. She would study them carefully and make sure she did nothing to violate any of the Wingarden policies until she did what she had to do.

Allowing the safety of Evie Wingarden to be compromised.

Well, that went without saying. She would never do anything that would harm Evie. Unless you counted abducting her for ransom. But Evie would *never* be harmed.

Non-performance of agreed-upon job responsibilities

She sighed deeply. She would make sure everything was done to their liking.

Breach of confidentiality clause.

Penny would make sure she would not breathe a word to anyone. She knew they would have her tracked and probably listen in on her phone calls so she would have to be careful. Very careful.

Smoking or consumption of alcohol while on duty or use of an illegal drug

That went without saying, of course. Penny gave up smoking a long time ago. And she only drank on occasion. She could do this. She could so do this. She wanted her money. She was going to get her money back.

Overuse of cell phone while on duty or while driving

Wait. What? Overuse of cell phone? Okay, she would *never* use her cell phone while driving. That was just stupid and dangerous. But other than that, she needed to have her cell phone with her at all times. Of course, she would keep her eye out on Evie at all times. But damn! Every millennial lived with their phone. It was like a conjoined twin. Inseparable. They probably should have hired an older nanny then.

Okay, she could do this. She could so do this. Her goal was to get her money back from Bianca and she was going to *not* screw this job up.

Unapproved guests

Unapproved guests? Did they mean she was not to have any boyfriends over? Ever?

She looked up at Vera who was eyeing her carefully. Penny gave her a reassuring smile.

"Everything okay, dear?" Vera asked, a smug expression on her face.

> "Yes, so far, everything's fine. I have no trouble with anything on the agreement." *In my dreams.*

"Good. It says a lot about you that you read over carefully anything you sign. This means you will take great care of anything concerning Evie and not cut corners."

"Thank you, Ma'am," Penny said, smiling politely, trying to hide the sheer horror she felt inside. Could she really do this? Could she pull this off?

She'd managed to change up her background information so they wouldn't know about her past.

She then read the last few items that would be grounds for immediate dismissal:

Stealing, dishonesty of any kind, any issues concerning background checks

Penny swallowed hard, her palms began to feel sweaty. She guessed kidnapping would fall under the stealing and theft category.

She tried to swallow but the lump of guilt, compliments of her conscience, wouldn't go down. Would Vera notice her nervous demeanor? The rich were good at sensing people. They studied people, didn't they? They were in positions of vulnerability and got into the habit or reading people around them.

After all, it wasn't your enemy who could betray you—it was a friend. Someone close to you.

"Everything all right, dear?" Vera asked again. "Do you have any problems with any of the items in the agreement?"

"Oh, no, Ma'am. Everything is just great."

Penny then read the last little bit about their social media policy. She would not be allowed to share any information about her location, her plans for the day or any pictures of Evie. She was not allowed to tell other nannies or anyone else, including strangers who she was or where she would be spending her time unless authorized by Vera Wingarden, Elvin Wingarden III or Bianca Wingarden.

She would also have a review at the end of thirty-days. Not ninety days like most contracts but thirty days to see if she would be a good fit.

Crap!

After all this, they could still easily terminate her if she was not a good fit in thirty days. Hopefully, she wouldn't need to be around that long. That would mean she would have at the *most* thirty days to come up with a plan to get her money back. She would find a way to take Evie Wingarden away from the Wingardens somehow.

She wanted her money back.

She signed and dated the form and handed Vera the papers. Vera then co-signed and dated the form as a witness and everything was set.

Little did Vera know that Bianca had stolen Penny's money in another life. She took Penny's life away. And Penny was going to get her money back, one way or the other.

Right now, Penny had to get used to a new reality. Penny was officially the new live-in nanny for the little billion-dollar heiress Evie Wingarden. Truth be told, she always loved children and would never bring any harm to them. Ever. She was just going to scare Bianca, the monster, into giving Penny her life back.

Today, she was Penny the nanny. But one day, they might call Penny the abductor.

12. Penny

The floor was expensive-looking, shiny oak with an intricate design. Penny could practically see her reflection when she looked down. Talk about immaculate. She guessed they probably had it polished everyday. There was no way they could keep this place so perfect without professional help, she mused.

Afraid to touch anything, she continued to walk through and noticed there were a few doors on the left side of the room.

"Go ahead," Vera prompted. "You can open the doors. One leads to your own bathroom."

"My own bathroom?" she parroted in disbelief.

Penny had never had her own bathroom before. She always had to share when growing up. She'd never known what it was like to have an en-suite. Never mind at the homeless shelter, where she had to share the bathroom used by everyone there. It was awful. Living with her roommate Bex in a closet-turned-room wasn't any picnic either.

Penny was stunned when she opened the bathroom door. She saw marble countertop and gold-plated finishing for the faucets. A deep soaker tub and beautiful trimmings.

Was she in a dream?

This could not be real. This could not be happening. She wanted to pinch herself but Vera was close by. She tried to hide her surprise. The last thing she would want Vera to think was that she was some nomad who'd never been inside a proper home before. To them this was life as usual. No wonder they fought to keep their wealth. It would be hard to go back to anything other than the best after a taste of elegance.

She noticed the toilet had an almost futuristic shape to it.

"Oh this is the new self-cleaning toilet."

"Self-cleaning?"

Did that mean she would not have to clean toilets then? She was half expecting little robots to come and clean around the house like those iRobot products on sale now. Then again, if she could remember correctly, when she'd read up on Wingarden's most elite clientele, they represented a lot of tech firms and organizations. She was sure they probably got free samples of their latest technology. Of course, they would have to if they were going to market the products in their department stores.

When she was done looking in the bathroom, she glanced inside the other door.

"Is this another room?" Penny asked.

A chuckle sounded from behind her. "Oh, no dear. This is your walk-in closet."

"Walk-in closet? This looks like a store."

Vera chuckled again. "My dear. This is where you'll dress in the morning and keep your things."

"Okay."

The room was also designed well with shiny hardwood floors and wall-to-wall shelves and built-in cabinets. It was immaculate. There was a window with blinds letting in the afternoon sunshine. It was grand, to say the least.

She noticed there were clothes already hung up. It looked as if they were right out of a store.

"Did this belong to your last live-in nanny?"

Vera cleared her throat. "Actually, these are your clothes, dear."

"My clothes?" Penny was horrified and part relieved. Firstly, she had no other clothes right now and she was terrified to have to spend her first paycheck on getting a new wardrobe to fit the job, knowing she would be seen in public with their child. But then again, how would they know her taste, her style, her size? Not that she hated what she saw at the moment.

"Do you like them, dear?"

"Yes, Ma'am. This is wonderful."

In her old apartment before Bex, she was used to old dirty pipes and stained countertops and cracked tiles on the floor. Nothing like this. She was even lucky if she got clean water out of the pipes. But that was then. This was now. This was her life now.

Until she got her money back from Bianca.

But a little voice inside her kept whispering into her mind: *Yes, this is good Penny. But how long do you think you will last here?*

"Oh, I almost forgot," Vera said. "We have a gift for you." She handed Penny a gift box.

"A gift? For me?" She felt as if she was on some reality game show.

She opened the box while Vera eyed her carefully.

"A new cell phone?" Penny asked, stunned beyond belief.

The rich really knew how to buy people. Her old cell phone had a cracked screen and was slow to boot. She couldn't afford an upgrade. How did they know?

"Yes, dear. It's a new cell phone." Vera's hand was oddly stretched out.

"Um, you want it back?" Penny asked confused.

Vera smiled. "Oh, no dear. You see, you will not need your own smart phone. Not while you're here. We'll keep it in a safe place for you until you leave."

Penny's heart squeezed. Her stomach muscles tightened.

That wasn't in the contract!

"Oh, um...really, you don't have to." Penny was lost for words.

"We *insist*, dear." Vera's tone had an air of finality to it. "It's for everyone's safety. You see this phone has a unique tracking device in case you are ever in trouble, we can get you help right away and of course, for Evie, who would be with you in your care. You can have your phone once you leave the premise on your own time for vacations and activities like that."

For vacations and activities like that?

Penny took out her phone and powered it down completely. She wasn't about to log into her email from her new phone. They'd be able to see every single thing. She couldn't risk that happening. She'd have to say her goodbyes to everyone and let them know she'd be unavailable while on her secret contract with the Wingardens.

She looked down at the new phone in her hand. It was a shiny gold-plated custom-designed smartphone with the Wingarden Family logo engraved on it. She'd read somewhere online that the Wingardens didn't use mass-produced smartphones, only smartphones specifically designed for them with heightened security features. There were no others like them in the world. She supposed it would make them less likely to be hacked.

Penny didn't know what to make of all of this.

"Is it set up?" Penny asked.

"Yes. It's already set up."

Penny observed the phone then carefully turned it on with a swipe of her fingers as per the instructions on the home lock screen.

Welcome Penny Andirs

Network: Wingarden WIFI

Passcode: ***********

"Oh, the default passcode is Wingarden 1906," Vera prompted.

"Thank you," Penny said, sheepishly.

Her heart galloped in her chest. She didn't know what to expect going forward. What had she gotten herself into?

No employer is going to pay you this amount of cash for nothing, a little voice of reason slid into her mind.

She noticed the pre-loaded apps. An app for weather, time, health stats, map, GPS, menu, trips, chores, activities, Evie's lists, important contact numbers, approved play list, approved movies, approved songs and so on.

She was going to ask what happened to the previous nanny, but she didn't have to now. The previous nanny probably quit on the first day to preserve her sanity—and her freedom!

As Penny continued to swipe the screen looking at all the pre-loaded apps, there was another one that caught her attention. It was an app that read: *Nanny.* She knew that was meant for her. She promptly tapped on the *Nanny* app's blue icon as Vera watched on, seemingly enjoying the spectacle of seeing her new employee fiddle with her new tech 'gift.'

The app had a colorful chart that illustrated how it tracked her hours, her movements, her location and the time it took her to do each task including bathroom breaks and how long she would spend in each area of the home including the shower, the kitchen, the play area and Evie's quarters—her play room or her bedroom.

It was tied to their main Wingarden Household server.

Penny's limbs felt weak with shock. *Holy shit!*

Her entire body tensed. Her heart thumped erratically in her chest. She swallowed hard, trying to hide her nerves. She was floored.

Were they serious?

She'd now began to wonder about her original plan and what the hell had she gotten herself into.

13. Bianca

If Bianca didn't know any better, she'd think her mother in-law and husband were trying to replace her with Mary Poppins here. Well, she was Evie's mother, and there was nothing they could do about that. They were not going to get away with it.

Her relationship with her mother in-law had gotten off to a rocky start. It was Vera who had insisted on having a paternity test when Evie was still inside her. They wanted to make sure the child was Elvin's before she was even born. Bianca never forgave her for that.

She didn't come from the right upbringing like his other girlfriend. Bianca was working class, if you include hustling as being working class. Still, they didn't know that. They would never know that. That wasn't good enough for Vera. Bianca even overheard Vera calling her a floozy once. Imagine that.

Bianca sighed deeply while Vera showed Penny "Mary Poppins" around the house.

"Where are you going?" Elvin said, coming out of the study carrying Porsche while Bianca walked towards the west garden.

"I'm just going out for some fresh air. Is that okay?"

"Of course. I didn't know how much you enjoyed gardening until recently. Why didn't you let me have Grant plant some flowers on the veranda?"

He meant the veranda to their shared bedroom—the shared bedroom where she slept alone while she slept in the other quarters with God knows who.

"It's okay. I don't mind going out into the garden. I don't want him working too hard."

"Nonsense. That's what we pay him for."

"The flowers are beautiful at this time of the year. I don't mind, really."

She had to remember that he could track her every movement through the damn apps on her phone. The ones installed by the Wingarden family. Everyone there was being carefully monitored.

Creeps.

Thanks to Vera. She was the one in control. Bianca still couldn't believe that witchy woman went through her private things in the attic and grabbed her old personal diary. That's got to be where she found the note.

Watch your back, Bianca.

If it were Elvin who found the rich husband list, he wouldn't be so nice to her right now.

"Are you happy with the new nanny?" he asked.

"We'll see how she works out."

"I'm sure she'll be fine."

"Yes, I'm sure."

Just then, the dog-walker came in. "Hi Flora, came to take Porsche out?" Elvin said.

"Yes. I just need to speak with you in your office for a moment. It's about the billing." Flora then turned to Porsche. "Hey there," she said, taking Porsche from Elvin's arms.

"Hey, Mrs. Wingarden." Flora then turned her attention to Bianca.

"Hi Flora. Thanks so much for taking him for a walk. I didn't have time today."

"Hey no worries. That's what I'm here for."

Later, Bianca met Grant, the gardener, in the massive garden near some pruned shrubs and trees.

"These okay for you?" Grant asked Bianca, handing her some flowers.

"Yes, they look fine." She stroked the beautiful flowers he'd just given her.

She then went into the gorgeous garden shed which looked more like a mini cottage surrounded by plants and shrubs with its own stone pathway and she took a look around.

She heard the footsteps of a man behind her. Then the door closed. It was dark in there save for some light coming from the sun roof and the windows.

He slid his arms around her. She leaned back into him.

It felt so good be in Grant's arms again. She hated that they had to hide. But she knew Elvin would have her out of there so fast if he found out she was unfaithful. Never mind his infidelity. Vera didn't give a rat's ass that her son was sleeping with everything under the sun with a skirt, including their precious dog walker, Flora. It was a double standard relationship.

"I miss you," he said, growling into her ears.

"I miss you too," she said.

"You're worried."

"How did you know?"

He took a joint out of his pocket and lit it. They shared a smoke. She had her perfume with her to get rid of the scent when they were done.

"Kiss me," she said.

He did and more. They made out in the makeshift bed in the back as they always did.

Bianca unloaded everything to Grant when she rested in his arms. As she always did. She just didn't trust Penny for some reason. She tried to tell Vera it was not a good idea to have a live-in nanny, but Vera insisted. At least she had a hand in choosing from the list of finalists. Or they might have ended up with a boob-job gold-digger.

Her husband, of course, the proverbial mama's boy, listened to everything his mother said. It was two to one. Not that Bianca minded getting a little help with Evie. She wasn't the world's greatest cook and it had been tiring, since she'd had a complicated pregnancy and Evie has a touch of ADHD. She wanted a break, not a live-in nanny. It wasn't easy caring for her child twenty-four seven without any support. Bianca knew she suffered with postnatal depression. It wasn't easy. Her husband was out a lot with his "secretary" and "dog walker" and they spent almost as much time together, if not more time, as Bianca and he did.

He offered her a drink. She took a sip and closed her eyes.

The Wingardens were planning to get rid of her. She knew it.

But she was going to get rid of them first.

14. Penny

The following day, as instructed by her Nanny app, Penny walked out into the massive garden at the Wingarden Mansion which looked more like a public park with its huge landscape and rows of shrubs, beautiful flowers, plants, trees and its own stone pathways. One could get lost in there.

She was to meet Vera, but couldn't see her anywhere.

The rows of beautiful flowers were stunning. Breathtaking, the scent of the pretty flowers wafted to her nostrils. She could hear birds chirping in the distance. She walked around mesmerized at the beauty.

"Well, you are a beautiful plant," she said to a plant. She had no idea what type of plant it was, but it was a breathtaking shade of purple. "I don't know much about flowers. Only roses," she said out loud.

Must be nice to have money like this that you could have your own palace and enormous garden complete with water fountains. After a few minutes, Penny turned around and her eyes widened in shock. She was stunned to see Vera standing quietly behind her, looking at her.

Where the *hell* did she come from?

Man, that woman was quiet. Penny didn't even hear her coming. Vera just sort of appeared out of nowhere. Had Vera been watching her this whole time? Okay, this was beyond creepy. She did not like how that woman behaved.

Well, one thing was for sure, if this family ever lost all their money on the stock market, Vera could always get a job moonlighting as a cat burglar. No one would ever here her coming.

"Oh, I'm sorry, I didn't know you were there," Penny said, shyly. How long had she been watching her?

"It's all right, dear. I see you've been admiring our garden."

"Garden? It's massive. It's like a forest. You could get lost around here."

Vera grinned and played with her pearls around her neck. "Evie will be with us soon. She's just finishing up her piano lesson."

Evie's piano teacher would be bringing her to them when she was done.

Penny supposed Vera wanted to take the opportunity to show off their wonderful garden.

Just then the gardener came out. He was young and handsome and built like an athlete, Penny noticed. He looked more like a male model than a gardener.

"Oh this is Grant," Vera said, introducing them.

Shit.

Penny's heart pumped harder. She recognized him. At least she thought she did. Where did she see him before?

Shit. Shit. Shit.

"Hey, nice to meet you," Grant said, stretching out his hand.

She shook it. A lump climbed in her throat. She swallowed. "Nice to meet you, too."

The gardener eyed her carefully.

"Have we met before?"

"Yes, when I came for the interview," she said, dismissively.

He laughed. "I meant before you came here."

"No. I don't think so."

Shit. His facial recognition was probably better than Bianca's. Shit. This could go crazy in a heartbeat if he knew who she really was.

It couldn't be him, could it? One of her ex's friends, some shady guy who grew a lot of weed. He was also a gardener and came from a family of landscapers. But no way could it be him. Besides, her ex's friend's name was Rod. Mistaken identity. It had to be someone else. Why would they let a guy like him work here? Then again, maybe Rod had a twin brother or something.

This reminded her that she was in the belly of the beast. On their turf. And if she got caught, she would be dead. There was no two ways about it. Buried under some cement in a basement in one of their properties.

An article she'd read a while back came sliding into her mind again. The headline played out in her mind over and over again. Of course that didn't occur anywhere in North America since many would never pay ransom as it would encourage the activity.

Ransom of $800,000 paid to nanny who'd abducted child in her care. Child unharmed.

Eight-hundred thousand dollars.

Penny's pulsed raced. She quickly swept that thought out of her mind.

Focus, Penny. You can do this.

Besides, it wasn't easy to just walk away with a child. Not these days. The Wingardens had cameras everywhere. Not to mention the cell phone had a tracking app on it so they knew her exact location. She was expected to keep their cell with her at all times.

Oh, they were good.

Penny looked up and thought she saw a shadow of a woman looking down at her. Did Bianca know? Did Bianca know who Penny really was?

No. She couldn't possibly know. There was no way in hell she'd allow Penny near her daughter or the home if she really knew.

"Evie?" Vera called out to the little girl who was walking down the stone pathway with her piano teacher.

Again, Bianca was not around her daughter, but Vera was the one in charge around the house. She must be the ultimate mother-in-law nightmare. Imagine having a child and a husband, but the husband's mother ran the show and told you what to do. Not to mention Penny now had to address Vera as Ma'am. Ma'am? In this day and age? Who did Vera think she was? The queen?

Evie came into the garden and stood looking at Penny. She gave a funny look and wrinkled her nose as if she smelled a dead rat as she eyed her up and down.

"Where's my iPad?" she yelled. "I want my iPad! You said I can get my iPad back!"

"Evie!" Vera's face reddened.

"It's okay," Penny said softly.

What was a three-year old doing with an iPad anyway?

"Salut, Evie! Comment ça va aujourd'hui?" Penny said cheerfully, remembering that they wanted to have someone speak French to the little brat.

"Your French is impressive," Vera said, looking pleased.

"*Ça va tres bien, merci.*" Evie's words were quiet and looked around for her iPad.

The little girl's response was very polite, Penny thought. She was learning well.

"*Je m'appelle Penny.*"

"*Salut, Penny,*" Evie said timidly and looked around for her iPad.

The gardener pointed out where it was and she grabbed it up and started playing on it. Her friend came from where she was playing nearby and sat down to play with the iPad, too.

She wondered why she was even there as a nanny. She sighed. At least she tried to connect with her. She'd try again.

She'd read that the little girl won some preschool French award and the family loved French.

Vera looked pleased indeed. "It's good that you converse in many languages with our little Evie. Some carers only speak in English."

"Oh, they need to have as much practise all the time so it becomes part of their vocabulary," Penny said.

She could tell Vera was impressed.

To the side, she saw Bianca on the balcony looking down. Bianca gave her a glare then went back inside through the glass French doors. She was dressed in a silky cream-colored gown.

What was Bianca thinking?

Was she going to try and set up Penny?

Penny had a month to impress Vera. She needed this job for at least a month—hopefully she would be done in ten days.

She hoped Bianca was not going to try and screw her over—again.

15. Penny

The following day, Penny sat in the Wingarden's massive garden on a bench by the tree, while Evie played with her friends.

She was still no closer to her goal of seizing Evie. She needed her money and her life back and to expose Bianca-not-her real name for the criminal she was.

If Elvin knew who he married, he'd have her arrested and locked away for good before she could do harm to anyone else. Bianca was a crazy fraud and she could turn on any one of them. Maybe that was her plot. Her plan. To slowly get rid of the family and keep the fame and money for herself. Though she'd have to watch out for her shrewd mother-in-law. Vera didn't look like the timid type.

So far everything had been uneventful. But it wasn't easy. It was a soul killing experience. She didn't mind the little kid, it was the restrictions placed on her that made her feel as if she was back in prison.

She had a few days left to do what she came to do. How was she going to pull this off? They had tons of events planned right now. Seemed like they had a full schedule every day of the week.

Every moment she was there, she was being watched. How was she going to go ahead with her plan now?

She had a few more days or a couple weeks to find out if she would make it past their thirty day trial period. She felt more like a product they were testing than a human being hired to sit by their spoiled three-year-old and be at her beck and call.

Evie had a piano teacher, ballet instructor, play therapist, private cook, and everything else at her beck and call. Penny was stunned to learn that Evie had a personal coach for her biking too. Why would a kid need a coach for having little bike races with her friends?

Of course, this was all documented on Bianca's social media posts. Or else what would be the point if the world didn't know how involved her little girl was?

Penny was just the figurehead nanny, to prove to the world that they hired a nanny to help with their little spoiled princess who had enough clothes in her closet that could clothe all the homeless children in the world.

She felt bad for calling Evie spoiled as it wasn't her fault her parents treated her like a freaking queen of the world who could do no wrong. *She was three years-old for crying out loud. Let her live like a normal kid!*

Penny spent time with Evie and her friends before they started playing around Evie's life-size doll house. She was instructed to give Evie some space. Imagine that? Just as long as she was in ear shot.

Still, it was a treat seeing the smiles on the children's faces and the carefree laughter.

She glanced at her Wingarden smartphone, resisting the urge to wave to the camera on the phone. She knew they were watching her. She glanced up at the French multi-paned glass door on the upper west balcony. She could see a shadow of a woman there.

It was probably Evie's mother, Bianca, watching Penny's every move again.

Probably wondering when she was going to make a move on her husband. But Penny had no interest in her husband, Elvin the third. She didn't do married men. Besides, Bianca had stolen her money, and she was going to get her money back. Though it was looking more impossible and difficult to pull off every day that she was there.

Penny glanced at her smartphone and sighed. Vera had explained to her earlier that she didn't want her nannies watching inappropriate or upsetting films so as to not tamper with their aura or energy or something like that. Only those with good energies could be around their precious little Evie.

How then would they explain Evie's weird parents?

Or was that the reason why they were not as involved in Evie's life behind the scenes, behind the social media photos, as one might expect?

She went onto the Wingarden Instagram page and saw all the lovely "approved" photos of Evie and Porsche smiling with the figurehead mother, Bianca. Sometimes Elvin was in the picture too. They got tons of likes and comments on what a happy balanced role model family they were.

Ha! If only their followers really knew.

The Wingarden couple were not really involved in Evie or Porsche's life. They had staff, or rather, Vera had staff to do *everything*. Since she'd been there for the past few days, Bianca had been doing nothing but glaring at Penny, watching her carefully and whispering about her when her high society friends came by.

Guests of the Wingardens would often praise the new nanny, but Bianca would say something snarky in response.

Penny just ignored it. She was just glad that Bianca didn't recognize her.

But then again, how would she? She stole Penny's money from her without even knowing who Penny was. Heartless bitch!

Penny wondered what the mighty Wingardens would do if they found out about Bianca's shady past—her other life. Her real character and the crimes she'd committed.

Penny tapped on the app on her new phone that read newspapers. She was careful not to read up on any articles like that fake-nanny kidnapping ring. A bunch of fraudsters posing as carers.

"You enjoying your job?" Mel, one of the elder housekeepers, asked Penny as she approached her while Penny sat on the bench, bored out of her head. They'd been introduced earlier.

"It's great, thanks. I love being here. Evie is wonderful." *A wonderful bag of trouble.*

So far, Evie had managed to get up earlier than anyone else, sneak into Penny's room take her things, smear her lipstick on the wall, and switch her tube of toothpaste for a tube of glue that looked like toothpaste.

How on earth did she manage that? She was an advanced kid for sure.

It took hours at the dentist to get rid of that trouble. She was sure Evie must have gotten help. She played pranks. Sometimes cruel ones and there was nothing you could do about it but smile and do her job.

Evie was nothing but pure trouble.

Bianca said nothing about it except that Penny had to be more careful or they may have to find someone suitable to handle Evie.

Of course, Bianca hit the roof when Evie stuck glue on her precious little Yorkie, putting stickers on the poor little pooch. She was close to giving Evie a hiding, but stopped when Vera came in. Penny had been on break at the time and Evie was supposed to be watched by another staff member.

She heard whispers that Penny might not be up to the job. But luckily Vera had defended her and said she was better than the other nannies. Penny shrugged it off as if she didn't care, but she'd have to watch her back.

"I'm glad you're here," Mel said.

"You are?" Penny said, surprised.

"Yes. The other nannies couldn't last long. Evie is advanced for her age. A genius maybe, but she's a handful. Lots of energy. Lots of pranks. We all have to be careful around here. For a while they said they wouldn't hire any more nannies, but Bianca's not mother material and couldn't handle her own daughter. Vera's in charge."

"I see that."

"Elvin. Well, he's just a little absent."

"You don't seem very fond of him."

"Not too many people are. He drinks too much. I loved the older Elvin, his father Elvin the second, and his grandfather. I worked for them. I watched how Elvin the third grew up spoiled. Didn't want to learn the business. Squandered money, slept around. He was so unlike anyone else. His mother just said their son was finding his way in the world. They argued a lot. That's why when the elder Elvin was diagnosed with the big

C, he knew at his old age it could be any time and he decided that he would not leave his fortune to his reckless son or his absent-minded wife."

"But Vera seems so on *top* of everything."

"*Now*, she does. Back then, she was all about the prestige. The money. Then she realized that her husband was right after all. Elvin, her son, wasn't managing the company well and sales started to suffer. He should have been able to forecast and bring the Wingardens Department Store into the future where online and digital sales are, but he didn't. He messed around a lot. But Ms. Vera would die before she left this beautiful place and lifestyle."

"So what happened?"

"Old man Elvin the second, told Vera that if Elvin had a child, everything would be left to the kid. But since he didn't at the time, it was all going to charity. Some private library out west."

So the rumors were true then?

"I see," Penny commented as if she'd never heard that before.

"So then Elvin was supposed to get with some heiress out west, but she never liked him and chose someone else. Then he married Lauraine, a simple girl from down south."

"Her name was Lauraine?"

"Yes, she was a pretty shy thing. Nice girl. She couldn't have kids."

"He must be paying some hefty alimony."

"Oh, no. She *vanished*."

"She vanished?"

"Well, they never found her body. They were out on the lake and she fell off the yacht."

"Yeah, I'll bet."

"Sorry."

"I mean, what a *regret*, he must have had. That he couldn't save her."

"Well, his old man wasn't leaving him anything. Only to a biological grandchild. So..."

"He did a Henry the Eighth."

"Some would say that. She couldn't have kids, so they separated for a while and got back together. And then some waitress at a club he slept with told him she was pregnant. She even announced it on her social media page, showed her pregnancy results and ultrasound images for tons of likes. The whole works. That's when his wife had her unfortunate accident on the yacht and died."

"Really?"

"Yes. Anyway, Bianca was determined to get him to marry her. And he said yes."

"And that's when they got married?"

"Not quite. I heard Vera made her take an in-utero paternity test to make sure it was his child. Bianca had it all there on her page like some reality show drama. Got a lot of likes for it. She became a social media queen overnight sensation. Revealing everything about her life."

Except her secret criminal past, Penny thought.

"Well, isn't that something," Penny said, trying to sound as intrigued as possible.

"You're telling me. So long story short, the child was his so they got married. But behind the scenes, we also knew there was a collective sigh of relief because old Elvin II decided to leave his entire fortune to the unborn baby on the baby's fourth birthday. Elvin II was an eccentric man. He loved the number four. It was his lucky number, he always said. Well, his grandchild would inherit half her fortune at four and the other half at twenty-four so that way her folks couldn't squander the entire amount before she reached adulthood and that way she'd have control over the rest of it. He got to spend time with Evie in her first year and he loved his little grandchild. She looks just like him. Large brown adorable eyes. Well, the board of directors are watching closely to make sure that Evie's funds are taken care of when she turns four."

"But what about now? What are they doing for money now?"

"Borrowed time, or I should say borrowed dime. They're counting on the inheritance to pay off most of their debts and all the bills they owe. They're living off the Wingarden name and reputation for now. And I think Elvin got some good money from his first wife's insurance policy."

For now, Penny thought carefully. Until she did what she had no choice but to do. She felt terrible that their little house of luxury cards was about to come tumbling down once she revealed who Bianca really was and got her money back.

Evie was worth a lot more than Penny thought. No wonder they put up with her tantrums. She was their golden child. Their meal ticket.

And of course, Vera wanted to make sure she kept the upper class lifestyle. Bianca and Vera hated each other. Vera figured once Evie turned 18 she'd have her granddaughter with her. If left to Bianca, she'd probably kick them all out. She was keeping the upper hand.

Interesting.

"Thanks for the heads up," Penny said. She enjoyed her little talks with Mel.

"Oh, no worries. I'm too old to care right now. They can't do anything to me. They tried to get me to sign some sort of agreement. I've been here since Elvin the first. Three generations. I'm in my eighties."

"You look very well for your age."

"Thank you. I take care of myself."

"You sure do."

Penny felt bad for what she was planning. But she had to go through with it if she was going to get her money back from Bianca. She knew she wouldn't last long in this job. No sane person could last this long.

"They're looking forward to lucky eleven," Mel added. "They'd probably get rid of me then."

"What's lucky eleven?" Penny asked Mel. "The eleventh day of the month?"

"That's right. You seem like the only one who cares about the child. I worry about the little girl. They can't wait until Evie turns four. They're an eccentric group. When she turns four on the eleventh, her birthday, she inherits the fortune."

Penny felt her stomach squeeze. Should she go ahead with her plan to abduct Evie? But she needed her money back. But should she wait until the eleventh?

She didn't have much time.

Bianca ruined Penny's life. She had to get back what was hers, before it was too late.

Evie was the only collateral that made sense. She'd be out of a job if they shipped Evie off to the private school. Who the hell shipped a four year old off to boarding school? They were clearly using the child as a pawn. Her heart tugged for the little girl. Which brought her to another question: why the hell go through all that trouble of hiring a live-in nanny? For school breaks and events? Just to add one more impressive employee on the bankroll, because all the other rich housewives have a nanny?

She would never harm the little one. She just needed her money. That's all. She was going to have to move faster. Change of plans.

But Bianca was popular with millions of followers. She was no small potatoes. Penny realized she would probably have to change her identity later—again. Bianca would kill her.

Shit.

Maybe she didn't think this through as much as she should have. But she couldn't give up now. No way in hell.

Bitch has my money.

I'm getting my money back.

Mel eyed her strangely for a moment. Did she suspect what she was going to do? Did she know?

Could Penny trust anyone?

The rich and powerful have a way of digging up all kinds of stuff on people, didn't they? They were notorious for surveillance of everyone who worked for them. Even had spies amongst the staff.

Trust no one.

Your enemies can't betray you—only a friend can do that.

A friend who's close enough.

She knew that all too well.

Then she thought: get yourself together.

The nerve of that bitch Bianca living the high life when she destroyed Penny's life like it was nothing. Did she really think she wasn't going to pay for that? She was delusional.

Her heart pounded in her chest. Could she do this? Was she delusional?

Penny had to talk herself into this. She had to go through with it. By the tenth. Or it would be too late.

She'd prepared for this role the whole time.

The world knew Bianca as the famous socialite, but Penny knew what Bianca was about. Penny could die exposing Bianca, but she had nothing to lose.

Nothing to lose.

Except her money.

Children are a blessing," Mel continued the conversation. "This line of work is good practice for when you start a family of your own."

"Oh no. I can't have children."

"Sorry to hear that." Her face looked crestfallen.

"It's okay. I don't want children anyway." She caught herself. "I mean, I...I love children. I...I love working with them...Don't get me wrong. It's just that..."

"I understand. Some people take it for granted they can have children. Well, you seem so great with Evie. You know you have the best rapport with her that I've seen since they started hiring nannies."

"Thank you. Well, it's not hard. Evie is sweet."

A lump of guilt climbed in her throat. She felt a squeezing feeling in the pit of her stomach over what she was about to do. Kidnap Evie.

But Bianca had her money and that was the only way.

Of course, little Evie would be fine. No harm would come to her. She'd see to that. But she knew cutthroat billionaires like the Wingardens would have her for lunch when they found out.

"Well, I'll be seeing you later," Mel said, getting up.

"Nice talking with you, Mel."

Penny sat for a while listening to the birds.

Penny's heart stopped beating. She got up from the bench. It wasn't what she heard, the birds chirping in the background, it's what she *wasn't* hearing, the sound of children laughing and playing.

The wind rustled the tree leaves. She looked around.

"Evie!" she called out.

She went to the play house. There was no one there. Penny went looked inside the playhouse. It was empty.

"Evie! Where are you sweetie?" Penny called out.

She felt a disturbing quake in her soul.

Evie was gone!

16. Penny

Penny searched around frantically, her heart pounding fiercely in her chest, her pulse racing.

Her cell phone beeped. She was leaving the approved zone area.

"Shit. Shut up, already!" She scolded at the phone.

She regretted saying that realizing that she could be recorded. Then a sick thought penetrated her mind. What if they were listening in on her conversation with Mel, their old housekeeper?

"Evie!"

Her breath burned in her throat.

Penny was dead. They would kill her if anything happened to their little girl.

Yes, she had planned to take Evie away from them for a while but not like this. Evie was missing. Penny's life was over.

What made her think she could take this elite group of power-hungry rich people on? Was Mel in on this too? Was she planted there to set Penny up? Did they figure out who Penny was or what she wanted to do?

Just then she spotted a doll on the ground beside one of the trees. She ran over to the object. When she leaned down to pick it up there was a note on the doll that read:

Ha ha.

Stupid?

She then felt a bucket of water pour over her. She was drenched. She screamed out in shock.

"Ha, ha. Stupid."

She looked up and saw Evie near a small tree house beside the tree that she'd climbed up to with steps built down the side.

"Evie, what are you...What are you doing? What are you doing up there?"

Just then Vera came charging through the grounds.

"What's going on here?" Vera said. "Evie get back down here at once."

"Okay, Grandma."

"I'm sorry about this," Vera said, apologetically.

"Oh, no. It's perfectly fine. She just wants to have some fun. I don't mind, really."

Vera scolded Evie then told her to get back inside the home. Her friends climbed down the treehouse too.

"I'm truly sorry about this," Vera said again. "You'd better get cleaned off and dried. We have a shopping excursion planned."

"Sure. No problem."

Was she serious?

Okay, now she was beginning to see why they made a two-week trial period. Nannies probably never made it past the first two weeks.

Evie came over to Penny.

"Hug," the little girl said to Penny.

Oh, no. Was this another trick? Okay, fine. She would take whatever was coming to her.

She leaned down and the little girl hugged her and Penny hugged her back. Evie kissed her on the cheek.

Aww.

"Thank you, Evie."

Evie then giggled and took out a squirt gun she was hiding.

Oh, boy.

"Well, that's different," Vera commented. "She never hugged any of the other nannies."

Maybe that was because Penny wasn't after her daddy. She really did love being around children. They had an innocent way about them. Nonjudgmental. Full of energy and love and fun. She wished her life was like that.

She realized the kid just wanted someone to let loose. Maybe that was it. Well, there was a time when Penny was a carefree spirit too. A long time ago. But Bianca took everything from her. She took her money. She stole her life.

Penny knew the Wingardens were probably going to let her go.

She'd already heard they were planning to ship Evie off to boarding school. So why would they need a live-in nanny? Unless they were planning to send Penny there too. She would never last in a high-security boarding school. They'd find her out.

But she still only had less than ten days to do what she came to do.

17. Penny

Later that afternoon, after Penny had dried off and changed, she was told to meet Bianca in the living room in the west wing.

The west wing?

The east wing was where they often socialized. The west wing was mostly for business. Like firing, probably.

Her heart pounded with ferocity. Every moment was a risk. When would Bianca recognize her? If she did, there would be no way out. As much as little Evie was a handful, she was a cutie pie. There was no way she would want any harm to come to her. None at all. But Penny had to follow through with her plan. She had to get the kid and leave first. There was no other way.

"We're going to a birthday party for Lady Rachel's daughter's first birthday this evening," Bianca told Penny, while fixing her lipstick in her compact mirror. She wore a pink tight-fitting designer dress. The scent of designer perfume oozed from her a mile away. "The party was supposed to be on Saturday, but there's been a change of plans. Besides, today's her daughter's actual birthday and they're flying off to Italy on Saturday instead."

If this was supposed to be a children's party, why the fancy adult dress up? Oh, right. This was supposed to be an Instagram moment.

Bianca was seriously trying to outdo Lady Rachel at her own child's party?

"Oh, how wonderful," Penny said, trying to sound enthusiastic, she pulled out her notepad on her Wingarden smartphone and began taking notes. She was told to take notes when spoken to for duties to be performed so she did not miss any important details. The family did not like to be asked about clarification. They preferred the staff to get it right the first time.

"Please buy matching outfits for Evie and Porsche that will match my pink Gucci dress. The Yorkie store is waiting for your arrival and the Baby Gems store has Evie's dress."

Was Penny supposed to be Bianca's gofer now, too?

This wasn't part of her nanny job duties, was it? She was a dog sitter now too?

"Sure, no problem." Of course it would be a problem. Penny finished jotting down the notes in the Nanny Notes section of the app.

Penny tried hard not to look at that massive red rose tattoo on Bianca's forearm. She tried to hide the overwhelming feeling that settled in her belly, reminding her of the trauma she endured the last time she saw that tattoo many years ago.

It was a good thing Bianca didn't recognize Penny. If she did, Penny wouldn't be standing there alive. If Bianca knew who she was, she'd kill her on the spot. Finish the job.

The Wingardens clearly didn't know who Bianca was. But Penny knew. Bianca was a dangerous criminal. A ruthless monster who had to be stopped. And she stole Penny's money. And Penny was going to get her money back if it was the last thing she did. Trouble was, she had a sick feeling it really might *be* the last thing she ever did.

"Lady Rachel?" Penny said, getting her mind back to reality.

She'd just realized Bianca mentioned they would be attending Lady Rachel's daughter's first birthday party. Like seriously?

How on earth did Bianca know Lady Rachel? Then again, money and rich folks mixed, didn't they? They all hung out in the same circles. Away from poor folks like Penny.

But oh, they wouldn't want to be around Bianca-not-her-real-name Wingarden when the truth came out.

Of course, she was being paid for her discretion so she could never talk about meeting the rich and famous during her employment with the Wingardens.

Still, Bianca hardly spent time with her kid. It was as if the kid was a prop. A gold ticket.

Poor kid.

"What's the spending limit for the party dresses?" Penny asked as polite as she could.

"If you have to ask, you can't afford it. The card has no limit." Bianca shot Penny an unreadable expression.

Penny looked away as if focusing on her notes on the app. She wrote down everything on the notepad she'd been given for her job. Furthermore, she wanted to avoid long eye contact, in case Bianca recognized her.

"Sure...Um...sure." Penny's heart squeezed with every beat in her chest. She'd better be careful not to misstep. Not to raise any suspicion. She'd be the good nanny. The compliant nanny.

Was Bianca trying to trick her? None of this was part of the Nanny Agreement.

Bianca scooped up her little Yorkie and hugged the pooch close to her after she was done touching up her makeup.

Penny had noticed that the living room had many family portraits mostly of Evie but equally tons of photos of little Porsche. She'd read once that Bianca had taken a private plane trip to Beverly Hills, California in the US to shop for exclusive items for Porsche. Her little pooch had a 22k Gold-Thread Pet Mattress that cost almost $2,000 according to Bianca's social media account. The dog ate out of a 22K gold leaf Borocco Pet Bowl by Versace. Her Louis XV Pet Pavilion pet bed cost $23,990.

Imagine that. Talk about one spoiled pooch.

In all fairness, she'd taken her daughter to Disneyland for a two-hour trip because she wanted to see Mickey Mouse in person that day.

The Yorkie barked a few times.

Penny kept track of all that money being spent from reading this woman's social media feed. She hid nothing from her followers. More like, she showed off to her followers.

That pet bed cost more money than most working-class people made in a year! The little pooch also wore Roberto Cavalli's line of pet clothes. Never mind the silky bow ribbons, Porsche had a 2 million dollar dog tiara—according to Bianca's social media page.

Like seriously?

She wasn't a prized pooch that won some dog awards or something.

And all this time, Penny thought the key to a happy dog was spending time with it, playing with it, getting exercise and just hugs.

Oh, well. What did she know?

Bianca's dog had tons of coats. Little Porsche had more clothes than Penny did and *she* was human—though she didn't feel that she was treated that way whenever she was broke!

She glanced at Porsche's parka jacket, a luxuriously quilted Parka Coat with a faux trimmed detachable hood.

Right now her pooch wore a British styled Woodland Country Jacket. Apparently some wealthy pets lived better lives that most of us could ever dream of. They had it all, from designer clothes, high velocity dog grooming dryers, diamond luxury dog collars, luxurious beds and accessories. Penny looked on in disbelief as she waited for the driver to pick her up for her chore. She glanced at some of the most ridiculously expensive products for pets ever made.

For folks like Bianca, it wasn't enough to be rich, you had to *show* the world. Once she even heard her talking to her friend about getting more likes and comparing likes with other socialites' media pages. How many hundreds of thousands of likes they had and fifteen thousand shares on a post.

Competition.

It was a popularity game to many of these rich chicks.

Who could get the most social-media-worthy moments and the most likes.

Live and post. Live and post. Live and snap and upload. Then repeat.

Penny resisted the urge to roll her eyes. Inwardly, she was burning up. Could she handle this job and keep her blood pressure down and her spirits up? That was going to be tough.

Right now, Penny had money on her mind. Her money.

Keep your eyes on your money, Penny. That's what it's all about. And don't get yourself killed.

18. Penny

The next day, Penny went on a little errand for Vera. She was instructed to look for Bianca, or Queen B as many in the household refer to her, in the massive multi-wing mansion. Vera said she couldn't find Bianca and needed her and Evie for a photo op for some magazine article featuring the Wingardens. A reporter would be there soon.

Couldn't she just call Bianca? Or was Bianca's tracking device cellphone turned off?

Even though it was the end of the summer holiday, the rich kids sure stayed up late. Penny still had a migraine after going to bed late after the party and having to wake up early this morning.

Still, yesterday's party was a blast, Penny had to admit. A bit over the top, but she tried not to be star-struck meeting Lady Rachel. Evie was well behaved, thankfully. She was also the best dressed toddler there, next to Lady Rachel's daughter, of course. Lady Rachel didn't seem to like that.

When she got back from the party last night, Penny overheard Vera on the phone saying how much she hated that Bianca displayed her wealth like "*new*" money. Penny guessed there was a divide between old money and new money. Those who were not used to it and when they got it they flaunted it like there was no tomorrow. Like literally, spending it on high-ticket items as fast as they could. And then you had Vera's lot, who obviously was a bit more discreet about it and were careful with every penny. And they certainly never flaunted it on the internet for all too see. Evie's dress was encrusted with diamonds with matching tiara as if it were her own birthday party.

Penny sighed.

Rich people's problem.

The corridors in the west wing were lined with more portraits than an art gallery.

She went to a room and knocked on the door. There was no answer. The door was opened slightly. She was tempted and decided to go in.

"Hello? Bianca?" she called out softly.

Couldn't Vera just send Bianca a text message or something?

When she walked into the massive room, she was floored. Her jaw fell open.

The room was a massive gallery of designer shoes. It looked like a grand ballroom with ceiling to floor rows of shoes.

This must be Bianca's Shoezeum she'd boasted about on her Instagram page. Bianca was interviewed by a woman's magazine and held the record for having the most shoes. Something like 2,500 pairs. Who needed that many pairs of shoes?

Penny walked into the well-lit room as the sun shone through. Glass and mirrors all over. The room was bigger than the house she grew up in.

The designer shoes were arranged in rows. Givenchy, Prada, Louis Vuitton, Nike, Dolce and Gabbana and Gucci shoes to name a few. Stilettoes, sneakers, leather boots, every shoe style under the sun. There was another room joined to that room with designer clothes and then another section for designer handbags. Again, all the top luxury brands like Luis Vuitton,

Hermes, Chanel, Valentino and Gucci and more to name a few. In all colors and designs.

There were paintings in the room and photos of Bianca wearing her sexiest shoes with barely anything else on except a silky slip dress as she posed seductively with her shoes. Then there were a few pics of her with her shoes and her dog Porsche. There was only one picture of Evie in the room with Bianca. No picture of Elvin. Looked as if they weren't that close.

Elvin was always away at meetings and was hardly home. When he *was* home, he was in the vodka bar—a lot. He was either there or at the pool house or spending an inordinate amount of time with the dog groomer, Flora.

He'd been kicked off the board, Penny had read. Rumor had it he was a drunk who messed up a lot and could never live up to his old man's name.

Looked as if Bianca was stuck with Elvin's wild ways and could do nothing about it. She probably wouldn't want to give up all of this luxury.

Each person in the Wingarden household had their favorite room. Evie had her play room or her life-size doll house. Vera loved organizing stuff in her office, planning networking and lavish events and ways to run the lives of everyone there. She kept most of her important events and thoughts in a massive pink binder. Her favorite color.

Elvin loved his vodka bar and man cave while Bianca loved gardening for some strange reason. Yes, gardening. Surprisingly enough, she was always around the gardener when he came by.

She recalled the time Bianca showed off her $50,000 Louis Vuitton handbag on her Instagram page. She once said her bag was her best friend. How strange was that? Seemed like she spent more time with her stuff than the people in her life.

Penny sighed deeply.

Must be nice to have deep pockets. And all Bianca had to do was push out a kid for a rich guy. A rich guy with old money, too.

There were pictures of her on one of their yachts dressed in strapless poolside dress, draped in diamonds sipping champagne with her luxury designer bag at her side while reading on her e-reader.

Show off.

Little did anyone know, but Bianca was a fraud. She was a criminal who would stop at nothing to get what she wanted. And she owed Penny big time.

Penny had struggled her whole life without food to eat most days or clothes on her back. She'd lived in and out of shelters and bounced from foster home to foster home after she lost her folks. She only spent a brief time with her grandmother until she passed.

She thought about the irony of it all. Bianca's past was dark and dirty. No one knew that. Bianca probably wasn't aware of what she'd done to Penny.

Looked as if Bianca had a big makeover, not just in her financial life but her in personal life too, in her memory. Maybe she altered her memory or hired some expensive shrink to hypnotize her into wiping away all the shit she'd done in her previous life, hoping no one would catch on to what a fraud she really was.

Bianca was a thief. She didn't deserve to be the richest housewife in the country. She didn't deserve any of it. Bianca had stolen Penny's money. And Penny came for what was rightfully hers.

Well, of course Bianca looked fabulous. She had a staff of a hundred people doing everything for her. She didn't even have to lift a finger to take care of her kid. Everyone else did that for her. No wonder Vera was in charge of everything.

All Bianca did was spend money. Some housewife. Maybe that was because she was a *rich* housewife.

"What are you doing in here?" A voice sounded from behind her and Penny's heart stopped. She turned around.

It was Vera.

Standing right there in the shoe room, not far from where Penny stood.

She had her hands clasped together. An unreadable expression on her face.

Holy shit! That woman could really sneak up on a gal. How long had she been standing there watching Penny?

"Oh, Miss Vera. I mean Ma'am. I'm so sorry. I had no idea you were... I mean, I thought Bianca would be in here..."

"It's quite all right, my dear. As you can see she's not in here."

"Yes, Ma'am."

Vera glanced around with a wrinkled nose as if scorning the room. She could imagine how she felt about her daughter-in-law's expensive habits.

"I will go and look for her now, Miss. I mean Ma'am."

"Very well."

Penny left immediately, almost getting lost in the massive walk-in closet or walk-in ballroom of shoes. Moments later, she found herself going down the marble stone stairwell to the west garden and made her way outside.

She walked along a garden pathway towards the west garden, but didn't see any sign of anyone. The birds chirped in the distance and she could hear the sound of the lake and the trees rustling in the late summer wind. It was quiet around there, just the sounds of nature. That suited her just fine.

Penny walked along the stone pathway leading up to the garage area pass the golden iron gates. Each area was gated it seemed. She inhaled the fresh country scent. It was nice to be away from the busy city for a change.

She saw the massive roadway to the 16-car garage and a small street sign reading Car Drive.

She smiled to herself. Must be nice to have such a huge estate that you could label every area with a private street. Their daughter had her own street and they even had a street for their luxury rides.

This all made Penny sick to her stomach or green with envy at how the other half lived. Still, she had to remind herself she was there to do a job.

She looked at the street with the open garages neatly organized and it hit her like a reality brick. That bitch had a 16-car garage? Seriously?

And they weren't cheap-ass cars, either. Each garage had a luxury ride parked cozily inside it. Two Porsche Panameras, a Bentley Bentayga, a Bentley Continental GT, a Range Rover, a BMW 7 Series, an Audi A8, Roll-Royce Phantom, Jaguar I-Pace, a Lexus LS, Mercedes S-Class.

These had to be among the top 10 luxury cars in the world right now, and they had them in their collection. It was as if they looked up the top luxury cars and made sure to have them in their garage to show off during their networking galas or walk-through tours after their lavish pool parties or gala events.

Who the hell needed *that* many cars? There were only four members of the family and one of them under the age of five. Like seriously?

Penny recalled the early days growing up when dad had to walk to wherever he wanted to or needed to go. They couldn't even afford bus fare at times.

And during the brutal winter storms, her father got frostbite waiting for the bus that never came in sub-zero degree temperatures like -40 degree wind chill. All to get to a low-wage job that barely kept the roof over their heads. No one would even give him a ride.

Today, Penny glanced around at the garage that housed their luxury vehicles realizing how the other half lived. These luxury vehicles didn't include their chauffeur-driven limousine when they wanted it.

But they worked for what they have, Penny.

Really? she wrestled with her inner voice. No, the Wingardens were handed their wealth like a luxury hand-me-down. Something they didn't have to work for or earn.

They lucked out in the gene pool lottery. That didn't take skill. It was the luck of the draw where you were born and whom you were born to and where you were born. Something people often took for granted. Still, she supposed she should be happy to be born in North America. At least she had a shot at getting ahead. It wasn't easy, but there were opportunities.

Bianca wouldn't be here if she hadn't snapped up her own opportunity, right?

"Well, looks like Bianca, the Queen B's really living the lifestyle," Penny whispered to herself.

She shook her head and narrowed her eyes. She had to keep her cool and keep this new nanny job as long as she could until she got what she came for.

She could not afford to be fired now. She had to get inside the Wingarden inner circle. She had to earn their trust.

She couldn't afford to turn back or back down.

What would the Wingardens think if they knew Penny had been a temp at the elite nanny agency and when they requested a nanny, *she* was the clerk who gathered a list of qualified applicants for the position?

It was Penny who deliberately put forth the profiles of the hottest-looking, talented nannies and then shoved her homely-looking self in the mix. Hoping, praying, they'd take the bait. Hoping they would select the homely non-threatening-looking girl.

And they did.

Penny grinned to herself.

She wanted this gig.

She had it out for Bianca and Bianca had no idea who Penny really was.

Penny had planned this moment for so long.

That bitch had Penny's money.

And Penny was not leaving this nanny gig without what she came for—and it wasn't just the fancy one-year salary.

19. Bianca

Bianca Wingarden switched on her phone—the device the Wingardens used to track her down, though they would never admit it. She tried to relax while the masseuse finished with her shoulders.

It looked as if her mother in-law was trying to get a hold of her earlier. She just wasn't in the mood to talk to her then.

She glanced at her social media page. She'd just gained a few more followers.

Her social media account had 20,134,302 followers. Of course, Amanda Darling had 22,252,000 followers.

Not that she was keeping track.

"You're tense today," Lin, the masseuse, said.

She sighed. "Got a lot on my mind," Bianca replied.

"You need to take it easy, Miss Bianca. Don't let anyone stress you out."

Bianca liked Lin. She was always in her corner and knew exactly how Bianca felt.

"We have a new nanny." Bianca's tone was flat.

"Oh, Ms. Vera hired another nanny?"

Lin knew very well who was in charge of the Wingarden household. But not for too long. Bianca had her plan and she was going to stick to it. Vera should be on her way out now. Bianca was the housewife of the Wingarden Mansion. Why was Vera still hanging around? Her husband was dead. Her son should be the man of the house, with Bianca running things. Not Vera.

Vera always had the final say with everything, sitting in her office on the main floor of the mansion, dishing out orders like a CEO to her executives. She ran everything like a business. Granted, Vera used to be the secretary to Elvin the II, then she got promoted to his personal assistant. Then the rest was history, as they say.

So it was ironic that Vera saw Bianca as a gold digger after her son's fortune when she could be seen as the same. No one knew what happened to Elvin the II's former personal assistant before Vera stepped in. Rumor had it that she suffered from food poisoning one day at work, while Vera happened to be working in the same office. Then the next thing you knew, Vera offered to step in to fill that spot since she knew about the executive office. A few months later Vera was pregnant with Elvin the II's love child. He married her and that was that.

Was that why Vera despised Bianca? Because she knew Bianca knew her game plan? Gold-digger, huh?

Well, it took one to know one, didn't it?

Bianca was willing to bet that Vera had her own little trophy wife checklist too. There were some people out there that had it as their life long plan. Men and women. Yes, young men, like the hot gardener she hired, were probably setting themselves up to be in the right place at the right time to hook up with a hot older woman—or older man if they were a woman.

She received a text message:

The charade is over. It will be all over soon.

The charade was over? Who sent this? She glanced at the sender information. It was from an unknown source. An uneasy feeling washed over her.

Was that from her mother-in-law? Did Vera send that text message?

She could not go back to the life she came from. She was not going back. No way in hell. She loved being rich.

She loved the lavish lifestyle, the carefree living. She loved being able to request her private jet to whisk her off to any luxury vacation she wanted across the globe to sit on the most exotic beaches in the glowing sunshine or on an elegant yacht in the Caribbean sipping champagne without a care in the world, while her staff took care of every area of her life—including staff watching over her daughter and catering to her every whim.

She loved being adored by her millions of followers on social media for living the lavish lifestyle and showering her with praise for how beautiful she was and how amazing her life was, how delicious her husband was, admiring her million dollar designer bag collection that included everything from Louis Vuitton to Chanel and Hermes all housed in two massive rooms in her home. The largest designer bag collection room.

She had another room that was as big as her old apartment for her shoes. Just shoes and nothing else in that room, 2,500 pairs of designer shoes. The Shoezeum, her followers dubbed it on social media. That picture she took and posted garnered 400,000 likes in an hour.

She enjoyed getting on a private jet with her friends to Manhattan where she shopped on Fifth Avenue, had lunch in the theatre district then took her private jet back to Canada the same afternoon like it was nothing. She travelled by private jet everywhere like people traveled by Uber.

That was her life.

She loved it all.

She was the richest housewife in all the country and *no one* was going to undo that.

She'd worked too hard for it. She'd carefully planned out her life and she loved having it all.

She was a rich housewife, philanthropist, doting mother, social media influencer who could do it all and who had it all and no one was going to take that from her. No one. She'd see to it.

Damn it. They couldn't get rid of her *that* easy. She was Evie's mother. Yes, Evie was the heiress, but she was still Bianca's daughter.

Vera used the fact that Bianca had suffered from postnatal depression against her and threatened to take everything away from her. It was true that she was a bit distant after Evie's birth. Her birth had done a number on Bianca's already fragile body. It didn't help that she had to undergo all those ridiculous tests while pregnant to prove that she was in fact carrying Elvin III's child.

She wished she didn't agree to the nanny. It looked as if Vera wanted the nanny to take over. Damn it! Why hadn't she protested? She'd signed a contract before the marriage that as she would become part of the Wingarden household she would have to abide by certain rules and expectations including confidentiality.

Could that contract even hold up in court?

Never mind that. She knew that Vera was one to have spies around the house, which was why she had to be very careful. They would find a way to get rid of her and keep Evie away from her. That was not going to happen.

"You really are tense, Ma'am," Lin continued, distracting her thoughts.

"I think Vera's trying to get at me with the new nanny. I picked her out of a few finalists, but I think Vera might have told her to watch me."

Bianca carefully deleted the text message on the phone, hoping Lin didn't see it.

She would ignore what Vera was trying to do. If Elvin knew, he'd be angry with his mother. He wouldn't want Bianca to file for divorce. That could cost him a fortune.

He'd married her so he wouldn't have to pay child support. And so he would have an heir before his father died. He wouldn't dare divorce her.

During one of their lavish dinner parties, she'd overheard one of his snobby high society associates complaining about the $80,000 a month child support payment he had to pay out to one of his mistresses.

There was one thing Bianca learned about the super rich. They were super cheap. Sort of. Well, $80,000 per month child support wasn't exactly chump change but the idea that one would rather marry someone they didn't truly love or stick in a loveless marriage so they wouldn't have to pay child support was ludicrous.

"Are you sure? She let you pick the nanny, right?"

"Yes, but it's still a trick. She narrowed down the list of candidates. I think she was planning to use anyone on the list that I picked."

She knew she sounded paranoid, but she couldn't help herself.

"Remember what happened to the Dareek heiress?" Bianca said.

"Oh yes, I remember. Such a shame, wasn't it?"

"Yes, it was. I don't want to end up like her."

"Oh, no. You won't Ma'am."

"How do you know that, Lin? I don't trust anyone right now."

She didn't want to discuss too much about the family business. She'd signed a contract. But Lin knew her before she'd met Elvin. She also proved herself to be trustworthy. There were few people she could actually trust from her past. Lin was one of them.

She remembered the Dareek heiress.

That was a hot scandal a while back. Some young woman married into a powerful family dynasty. She'd given birth to the heir and then they found ways to get rid of her. It was worse than working for a company that fired you if it wasn't a good fit.

Dinereena Dareek's body was never found. They said she'd fallen off a yacht. But everyone said there was conflict between her and the elders in the family. She was seen as too carefree. Wild spending and partying.

She was used for her womb. Nothing more.

Many of those people in that circle would rather get rid of a trophy wife than divorce. Cost was always a factor. They wouldn't bear parting with half their hard-earned fortune.

She cringed at that notion. She feared Vera. She hated her. She didn't like the cold shoulder Vera had been giving her lately.

Vera took over her son's place on the board and had some control of the company. The board members loved the way she was so organized. Well, Bianca was about to change all that. She had to figure out a way to get rid of Vera first.

20. Bianca

Bianca had just finished up her wonderful massage and felt much more relaxed, especially after unloading her frustrations to Lin.

She saw on her cell phone under the Nanny app, that Penny had been in her freaking closet. How dare she? According to the app, she was in the closet for ten minutes.

Ten minutes? What the hell was she doing in there—and for so long?

That was Bianca's private place in the mansion. No one was allowed in Bianca's closet except Bianca.

Was she looking around at what she could take?

Bianca was going to have to keep a close eye on her and keep inventory of her valuables to make sure nothing went missing. Ever.

Or she'd end up going missing like the last nanny.

The last nanny was an au pair who'd come from a foreign country. She had been spending a little more time with Elvin than Evie, and Bianca hated that. It was a shame that the nanny drowned in the lake even though she was a swimmer.

Anyway, luckily, they were able to pay a huge amount to the nanny agency and to the family of the nanny and all was kept quiet. The family was so poor and grateful for the generous compensation which included a mortgage-free home.

The family used a company called Jackston & Jackston. They were known as fixers and public relations specialists. They were paid a handsome salary and hefty bonuses and earned every penny.

The Wingardens couldn't afford to have anything go wrong that would taint their image in the media. The board members would not be too happy if stocks tanked because of a scandal. But they knew full well that sometimes accidents happened.

"Where to, Ma'am?" Bianca's driver asked.

"To the house," she said. Though many would never refer to the massive mansion as a house. Vera had left her a text that the interview with the woman's magazine would be later and that she was to be there for the photographer to take photo. Something to do with the anniversary of Vera's mother in-law's death and how much the women in the Wingarden family held things together. Well, that was a laugh.

The phone rang and disturbed her daydream. It was Vera.

"Hello, Ma'am." She tried not to roll her eyes. Even though she was in the limo, the driver was a devoted family employee who'd been working for the Wingardens long before Bianca came along.

Vera sounded frantic.

"Bianca have you seen my pink binder with all the details of the gala event coming up?"

"No. Why would I touch it, Vera? I don't go into your office unless you're there."

"Oh."

Silence on the phone.

"That's very strange. Nothing has ever gone missing before in my office. I know where I place every item of work."

"Hmm. That's odd. Did you ask the new nanny?" Bianca tried not to sound sarcastic. "She seems to like wondering the hallways when she's not with Evie."

"No. I...I haven't."

For the first time Vera seemed unsure of herself.

Good.

She knew how long it took her to put together that silly binder for her presentations. She didn't like doing things on computers. She loved organizing things in her pink special binder.

Bianca was hoping for a way to get rid of Vera. Let her think she was losing her marbles. Now, she could blame it on the help and get rid of Penny too. She didn't trust her.

"I'll look for it again."

"Okay, Vera. Good luck. I hope you find it soon. I'll be there shortly." She tried to sound as polite as she could.

Vera was never going to find it. She was going to be losing a lot more soon.

21. Penny

"In breaking news, another child is missing this week," the reporter began on the twenty-four hour breaking news channel.

Holy shit!

Why was the TV in the play lounge on that channel?

Penny's heart thumped hard in her chest.

They were on to her.

They had to be.

Penny sat frozen while Evie played.

Evie had just finished taking photos for a magazine article with her mother and grandmother. Three generations of Wingarden women. Penny thought she'd be tired, but she couldn't wait to play. The TV had been on a children's channel and then it had suddenly flicked to the news station. Was Vera behind this?

No, it had to be Bianca, right? She sensed something going on. Bianca must have found out what she was about to do to get her money back.

Shit. Shit. Shit.

That little witch.

Just then, the TV station flicked back to the children's channel.

"Sorry about that," Bianca said over the speaker. "Please go back to your play."

Shit.

That was not a mistake. Penny acted like nothing unusual happened. Evie continued to play with her dolls while Penny engaged with her with enthusiasm.

She's watching you, Penny. Act as if everything's okay. It was the news after all. Maybe it was a coincidence.

Or maybe it wasn't, a little voice said inside her mind.

Later that afternoon, Evie went to take her "beauty" nap as Bianca had instructed on the schedule.

Earlier, Evie spent time with her cycling coach to ride her bike around the yard as if she were training for the Olympics or something. Penny thought that was the oddest thing for a three-and-a-half-year-old. Though Evie was tall for her age, and seemed like a ball of energy and fit, but still. Why on earth would Evie need a cycling coach? Like seriously.

Penny then went down to the west wing living area to see if she could speak to Vera.

Vera was having tea with her society friends. She was speaking to her friend, some Gloria woman. She'd overheard Bianca calling her Gossiping Gloria once.

"Another nanny kidnapped the child she was caring for. She decided to leave with more than her pay." Gloria commented. "How well do you know your nanny?"

"Oh, Gloria. Our live-in is perfect. Heavily screened."

"You sure now?"

"Of course."

She glanced nervously around and saw the look of shock and disgust on the pretty Botox faces of her other guests.

Penny wanted permission to leave the premises to go to town. She needed to get some help from a friend. She was wondering if she would be able to leave. She could always lie and say she had an urgent appointment. But then they might wonder what type of urgency was there. She was supposed to be fit as a fiddle and well able to take care of her charge, wasn't she?

"Excuse me, Ma'am. So sorry to trouble you."

"Oh, no problem, dear. What is it that you want?"

"Evie is fast asleep in your room for her nap. I was just wondering if I could leave the premises for an hour. I have...an appointment."

"What kind of appointment, dear?"

That's none of your business.

Think, Penny, think.

"My eye doctor. I...I need to sort out my new pair of glasses. These are tight."

She didn't seem too convinced.

"Couldn't you do this another time?"

What?

"It's all right, Mother. She should be able to take some time for herself." Elvin the third came out with a glass of wine in his hand. "You may leave to go to your appointment," he said.

Well, thank God for that.

"Thank you, Sir. I promise I won't be too long."

Well, it looked as if she'd misjudged Elvin the third. He seemed like an all right guy. No wonder he drank a lot. Having an overbearing mother who controlled every aspect of your life and a deceitful wife. Ugh.

She couldn't wait to get out of there.

Penny listened in on the ladies conversations while she grabbed her coat from the coat room.

"It's a shame, isn't it?" a friend said to Vera.

"Yes, it is." Vera agreed.

"You're telling me. Seems like we need to hire security for our children these days." The woman said in a heavy accent.

"Oh, I already have. We have nanny-cams around the house and outside so we have tight security. She won't be allowed out with Evie by herself. We're going to have security with her."

"Good for you, Ma'am," the friend said to Vera.

Penny felt her heart plunge and her stomach twist into tight knots.

More security? Nanny-cams? Didn't she mean *spy* cams? Hidden cameras placed strategically around the premise without the nanny's knowledge.

Well, that was crazy.

You want to deter anything from happening not *catch* it. Why not just tell the damn nanny so she didn't try anything stupid?

Penny felt deflated.

What was she going to do now? She would have to be very careful from now on.

Those crafty people. She should have known she wouldn't be paid six-figures and given access to their personal property without close surveillance.

Yeah, welcome to the lifestyle of the bitch and famous.

Not that she'd planned to do anything dodgy right now, but talk about lack of privacy. They didn't even warn her in advance.

"Oh, yes. I don't take any chances," Vera continued. "Besides, my daughter-in-law is not exactly mommy material. She really needs the help," she said.

Her friend laughed.

"No, really. Bianca's not coping well with all her duties. She certainly needed a little help," Vera added, probably not wanting to sound like the evil mother-in-law.

Okay, so it wasn't easy seeing her only son marry so quickly. But she knew that he wanted to end their brief fling. And then Bianca lied about her birth control and got knocked up. Vera knew her son would do the right thing and make an honest woman of her.

She was protective of Elvin. He was the heir to a billion-dollar dynasty. She couldn't be too careful with gold diggers. Penny had overheard Vera talking about Bianca and how she wished Elvin had chosen someone else with good breeding from a prestigious family line.

Good breeding?

So humans were dogs now?

"You have to be careful with these gold diggers," Vera's friend said beside her. "They'll trick the guy into thinking they're pregnant. Or carrying someone else's child."

"Oh, no. I made sure that could never happen."

"How?"

"I made sure she did an amniocentesis paternity test just to be sure the child she was carrying was his. And it was. I know Bianca hates me for it, but that's too bad."

Penny's eyes widened as she continued to listen in from the coat room, pretending to be fidgeting with her buttons on her coat.

"Amniocentesis? Isn't that risky?" her friend said.

"Yes, but I'm not taking any chances. At least we were sure it was his. Darling little Evie." She gushed over the portrait over the fireplace. Penny could see from the coat room since the living room doors were slid open.

"You seem sorry they got married."

"Well, it couldn't be helped. He knew we were to approve of anyone he marries, but..." She shrugged. "She was carrying his child so..."

"I see. How is she as a daughter-in-law?"

"She's okay. Spending my son's money like tomorrow will never come. And those shoes. How many pairs can she wear in a lifetime? Someone should have told her it's okay to wear the same pair more than once. She buys expensive shoes then wears them once and buys another. And they are so expensive. I told her the board won't like her display of wealth like that. She posts so many pictures on her social media page. It's sickening. Flaunting it like that. Leaving nothing to the imagination. She's lucky no one has made a kidnap attempt on her daughter to try to get ransom."

"Oh, tell me about it. Look at what that nanny did."

"I know."

"My daughter-in-law is the same way. Showing off. She's so *new* money. No class."

"Oh, you don't have to tell me that," Vera sighed deeply.

Penny tried to keep herself hidden while she listened, hoping Vera wouldn't notice she hadn't left yet.

It was clear that Vera hated Bianca. It looked as if Bianca took advantage of her precious baby boy to get to his fortune. Vera's fortune. Whenever she passed to the other life, her son and whomever he was married to would inherit everything she owned and worked for—or what her late husband worked for.

But it looked as if Vera worked hard behind the scenes to keep the estate running.

Vera continued, "He told me, 'Mom, she's carrying my child. I need to do the right thing. We need to get married. I can't have an illegitimate heir out there carrying the Wingarden name. Like it or not, she's a part of our family now.'"

Vera looked as if she felt a wave of nausea sweep through her. *Like it or not?* Yes, like it or not Bianca *was* a part of their beloved family line. The Wingardens were the closest thing to royalty in North America.

Bianca was a gold digger—and a con artist who stole Penny's money just as she was going to steal theirs.

The only thing keeping Bianca and her son Elvin together was the child. And Penny rarely saw them together. She did see them with other people, though. Bianca was sneaking behind his back with the gardener. And Elvin was out in the open with his indiscretions. As if he couldn't care less. It was as if they had an open marriage.

Vera told her friend that she didn't get the clear details of what went down, but according to Melanie, a shoe heiress, his other girlfriend at the time, Elvin had a bit too much to drink that night and long story short, he didn't come back to his hotel suite to be with Melanie. He was with Bianca, the waitress. The home wrecker turned housewife.

Vera had warned Elvin not to do anything foolish to ruin his wonderful relationship with Melanie.

Bianca had him trapped, Vera continued her conversation with her friend, and even if they ended up divorcing now, he would still have to pay six figures a month in child support, like what his cousin in California was forced to pay, so that she could live a lavish life of wild partying while leaving her daughter in the care of any Jane Doe.

Penny's stomach tightened into knots. Poor Evie. She was a pawn in all of this.

"There are some sick and twisted people in the world. But still, it's a good thing that good people outnumbered the bad by far. Or we'd all be in trouble."

Talk about awkward.

Vera would know that Penny overheard her conversation if she didn't leave soon.

She had always been untrusting of her surroundings. She was used to being followed. It was the story of her life. Especially with what happened in her past. But it was time to leave now. She had to get into town quickly and do what she had to do.

"You okay?" Penny's friend Dee said an hour later when she got into town. Actually, Dee was not much of a friend, more like someone she'd met a while back who knew her crooked late husband, Rexton.

Dee had her own little stall at a market in town. She had jet black hair and heavy black eyeliner and tattoos all down her arm and she didn't mess around. She sold all kinds of gadgets. Like watches and smartphones.

"Not really," Penny said, looking around, wondering if she were being watched.

She knew she couldn't have her own phone while working for the Wingardens but right now she needed some sort of system of help if she needed it there. She had a feeling she might end up cornered without a way out.

"You look like a bundle of nerves, girl. What's up with you?"

"Listen, I need a favor."

"What kind of favor?"

"I need a new watch. It's a gift. For a friend."

Her friend eyed her with suspicion. Okay, she was busted. There was no hiding from Dee. She'd have to spill the beans.

22. Penny

Later, Penny returned to the mansion. After Evie finished her short beauty nap, she had her piano lesson.

When her lesson was finished, she came running down the hallway toward her play room. That poor little rich girl sure had a busy schedule.

Penny asked Evie how it went after her piano teacher left, shaking her head.

"No! I hate piano. Go away." Evie huffed and folded her arms across her chest.

"Evie, be nice," Bianca said, walking into the play room.

"No!"

"Evie!"

"No!"

"You need to practise for your entrance exam."

"Entrance exam?" Penny asked, incredulously.

Evie ignored her mother, while Bianca ignored Penny's question. Vera came in and took over. The child seemed to listen more to the grandmother than her own mother.

Interesting.

Vera really did have the upper hand in the house. She wondered how it made Bianca feel.

Her mind thought about the pressure this poor kid was under. They were forcing her into some luxury preschool. An Ivy League preschool program. Instead of playing with blocks or other fun toys, the kids would be on a strict schedule at the new school.

They were paying big bucks so their kid could learn a second language by the time she was four years old or master the game of chess or something. The school was building little geniuses, but it was all about the image. Not just the company image but the family image. Getting their child into the best, most prestigious programs was a rite of passage.

Social proof of acceptance.

A stamp of approval based on the opinions of people who didn't matter. Well, maybe that wasn't quite true. The people who mattered could open more doors for their child and ensure the status quo. Hence the saying that the rich get rich and the poor get poorer.

She heard the tuition for the luxury program that offered the highest form of preschool education and nurturing for the aspiring moguls cost around $20,000 a month. Well, Evie was the heir to a billion-dollar fortune.

"Oh and by the way, Penny," Vera said in front of Bianca. "I'd like to commend you on the work you've been doing with Evie. We're very pleased with your performance so far. Just another week before the assessment. I think everything should be fine."

"Thank you." Penny tried hard not to beam. But this was good news. This was fantastic news. She would need more time to pull off what she wanted to do, but she couldn't do it just yet. She'd need to gain some more trust.

Bianca's expression was deadly. Good things looks couldn't really kill.

Later, Mel the housekeeper came back into the kitchen when Penny grabbed some healthy snacks from the fridge for Evie.

"You're doing well," Mel told Penny.

"Thanks. I'm trying."

"I think you just might make it."

"Make it?"

"Yes. They don't last too long here."

"What do you mean?"

Penny found it remarkable that Mel opened up to her, a virtual stranger when she hadn't been there that long when you consider the other staff members who'd been there for years.

"They've had many nannies before. But, well, one of them from some European country came here and had an accident and drowned just before her one month. Another one had an unfortunate accident like someone left some acid around. It was awful. Another left after the first day!"

"The first day?"

"Yes, she didn't get along with Bianca. I think Bianca didn't like the way she looked. The nanny looked like a model. And I think that nanny didn't like the fact that she couldn't keep her smartphone with her. You know, things like that."

"Oh, I see," Penny felt deflated. What was going on there with their nannies? Were they planning on setting her up too?

If that was the case. Penny had little time left to do what she had to do.

She was going to get her money back. And that was that.

23. Penny

You don't know who to trust with your kids.

That's why the super rich have cameras and security everywhere.

Silly parents installed nanny cams without telling the nannies. But that was wrong. You need to let them know the cams are around so that to deter the activity—not to catch it. Who wanted to see a video of their child being abused? Prevention was better than cure.

Of course, Penny was not one of those nannies. She was a good nanny. At least in her own mind she was. Everyone was good in their own mind.

It was a *self-serving bias,* as psychologists often termed it. It was a cognitive or perceptual bias that was often distorted by the need to preserve one's self-esteem so people saw themselves in a more favorable light.

Her phone rang. She glanced at the display screen. It was three-year old Evie calling to have pick her up from the doll house outside. A warm smile crept on her lips. She hated to admit it, but the little girl was too cute for her own good.

She'd told Penny earlier that she wanted some privacy with her little friends. Penny didn't know what the hell for, but it was her job to be on call. She was never too far from Evie and there were security outside roaming the estate discreetly. The more she stayed there, the more she felt as if she was in prison.

After spending time with Evie, it was her bedtime and Penny made sure that she was tucked in her bed, her plush toys at her side. She'd just finished reading her a bedtime story. Her job was done for tonight.

She glanced down at the list they'd given her to make sure everything was done the way they'd instructed. She crossed her T's and dotted her I's. They were very specific on how they wanted things to be done there. And at the generous pay she was getting, not to mention the sweet roof over her head, she didn't mind one bit.

Item number 14: Turn on the Disney nightlight.

She promptly reached over and turned on the nightlight for Evie. She then switched off the main light in the room. It illuminated in a nice warm glow. She hoped the child would be able to sleep soundly. She'd read up on the effects of sleeping with a nightlight, but it was what they wished and Evie was probably afraid of the dark like most children her age.

After she turned off the light, she noticed another spy camera on one of the dolls sitting on the dresser. There was one on the mirror too. She'd worked for a security company once in her other life, and could spot spy cameras.

There were times when it wasn't obvious because the cameras would be well concealed, but these gadgets were not as sophisticated. Or perhaps they wanted the nannies to know they were being watched at every turn.

She glanced at the photos in frames on the dresser.

Evie looked so adorable sitting on her mother's lap as they posed for what looked like a studio photo. There was another picture of Evie as a newborn. She really did have her mommy's eyes and her mommy's cheeks. What an adorable little thing.

Then there was a photo in a gold-plated frame with Evie and her grandmother and Evie's father. Bianca was not in the photo. How strange. Perhaps Bianca was the one taking the photo at the time. Who knew?

It looked as if Vera took quite an interest in her son's life and family. But then again, she was a doting grandmother, wasn't she? Still, the pose made Penny feel slightly uncomfortable. Vera leaned into her son as if she were his wife holding the baby. She didn't seem like the grandmother here in the scene. One would think she was the wife by the way she posed with her son and his child.

Penny wondered if Bianca took the photo after all. For some strange reason, she just thought it was bizarre family dynamics. Seemed as if Vera had more say in the family and in little Evie's life than the couple themselves.

The sound of a woman clearing her throat startled Penny and caused her to jump.

It was Vera standing in the doorway. She had an unreadable expression on her face. She wondered how Bianca felt about her mother in-law just appearing everywhere at random. How long had she been standing there? That sneaking little woman.

She'd go crazy if her mother-in law was forever in her home. Not that she knew what it was like to have a mother in-law.

"Oh, hi Mrs....I mean Ma'am."

Vera stood there, her hands clasped together in front of her. "When you're finished in here, I'd like to speak with you in your quarters."

Uh-oh.

Penny wondered how long Vera had been standing there watching her as she looked at the pictures on the dressing table. The woman certainly had quiet footsteps.

"My quarters?"

"Yes, in your room, dear."

"Yes, Ma'am," Penny said.

Vera left the room and Penny felt a slight chill in the air for some reason. She wondered what she'd gotten herself into. She felt as if she was back in prison for a moment. Always monitored by the security and guards. Watched.

Penny applied for the job to watch their little girl; she didn't apply for the job to be constantly watched. Or was that part of the job?

She let out a breath she didn't realize she'd been holding when Vera caught her gaping at the photos. She wondered what on earth Vera would want to talk to her about now so late at night—and in her quarters.

After Penny finished in Evie's room, she closed the door, careful not to make a sound. She then walked down the long corridor toward her quarters. Just as she was turning around the bend, she heard the muffled sound of a couple talking, or arguing. It was Bianca and Elvin. She thought she heard her name called.

"I don't trust her," Penny overheard the woman say.

Don't trust her? Don't trust who? Penny? Or Vera?

The man argued that there's nothing to be afraid of. "She's perfect," he told the woman.

"Perfect?" the woman answered back, dismayed.

That was all Penny could hear as she made her way to her own room.

Once she arrived in her room, Vera said, "I was just making sure everything is to your liking."

"Yes, it is. Thank you."

"Listen, I was just wondering, have you seen anything suspicious around here?"

In here? Fort Knox?

"No. Why?"

"I see." She played with her pearls around her neck. "It's just that I've been missing a few things lately and I'm not sure what happened. We have lots of staff working here, contractors too, as you can imagine. But my late husband never wanted cameras in the home so we don't have any."

No cameras in the home? Yeah right.

That was bull shit and she knew it. They had spy cameras or nanny-cams around Penny like there was no tomorrow.

But Penny said nothing and just listened. So they were hoping to catch Penny doing something stupid, huh? Was that what happened to the last nanny? Were they eliminated from the reality show called the Wingardens?

"Do let me know if you notice anything," Vera said.

"I will, Ma'am."

She felt an odd energy linger between them.

"Oh, and this Sunday, Evie will be participating in the Bakeroo Toddler Cup."

"The Baker what?"

"The Bakeroo Toddler Cup. Oh, never mind we'll explain on Sunday. It's going to be a busy weekend. I just want to make sure you're prepared."

"Of course, Ma'am."

Holy crap. Evie's had the schedule of a CEO. How was it this girl never rested? It was coming to the end of summer holidays, but this kid would be burnt out by the time she hit school in the fall. She would be turning four soon.

Still, she thought it was odd that Vera just happened to want to speak to her about all of that now. Was there another reason? Did Vera not want Penny to see something on Evie's dresser?

She'd keep it to herself for now. She could tell that Vera didn't trust her. What the hell did she mean stuff was missing? She should ask her thieving daughter-in-law, Bianca, not Penny, the nanny. Were they trying to set her up to take a fall?

Every moment she was there, it was looking more impossible to do what she had to do. But she had no choice. Maybe the Bakeroo Cup would be the perfect opportunity. Time was running out.

24. Penny

"A toddler bike race?" Penny asked Bianca on Sunday morning, trying to hide her astonishment. They were in the living area discussing the events for the day. So that's why Evie had her own cycling coach. No wonder Evie had been practicing on her bike every day since Penny had arrived.

"Yes, the Bakeroo Toddler Cup," Bianca explained. "Evie's been training hard these past few months."

"But she's only three."

"Yes, I know. She'll be four soon. It's good for her to start early in life. Life is a competition you know."

"I thought life is an adventure."

"Yes, that's what I said."

"Well, competition and adventure are two different things."

Bianca gave Penny a scathing look that made her realize she'd said too much. After all it was her daughter. She could enrol her daughter in whatever sporting event she wished, right?

"Sure, well, I'll make sure Evie's ready."

These rich folks seriously made their kids compete so early? Penny bet Bianca was only doing this for social media likes and picture-worthy posts to be shared.

Yes, it was a competition all right. A competition for rich housewives to show off their brood and prove they were superior to anyone else.

Penny was so glad she was not a rich housewife or trophy wife who barely interacted with her husband or her child and when they did interact, it was for the show-and-share online world.

Her husband was always too busy away from the estate on "business" trips to give the impression he was still important to the Wingarden empire. In fact, he'd been off the board for a while and was only working in minor roles. He was using the name recognition and the brand to get his way around town and to lure in more investors for businesses he had on the side. Rumor had it, he felt the Wingarden Department Stores was going to go the way of Sears soon and he wanted to ensure he had something else in the works as a backup.

Still, Penny couldn't worry too much about their messy personal life. She was on a mission. She was there to get her money back from Bianca, but she had to figure out how. The only way was to safely take Evie and make sure no harm came to her. But she needed her money back.

Would the race provide the best escape plan? But how would she do it?

The family arrived an hour later at the Water Fountain Resort grounds. Penny gazed around. How would she manage to take Evie after the race? There was so much security. Maybe this wouldn't be the best place after all.

Right now, she'd do her part as the doting nanny.

The race was quite an experience. Penny never knew events on this level even existed. All the proud parents, grandparents and friends came out to watch. There were over a hundred tiny competitors, all from well-to-do families, sporting their parents' or grandparents' company logo or family logo.

Yes, the family logo. Penny wished she knew what that was like. Having togetherness in a large family that was so well known that you even had your own logo.

The Wingarden family color was yellow with an emblem of a carnation, same as the Wingarden Department Store brand, and little Evie wore her yellow Wingarden T-shirt with the number 3 on it. Yes, three because her father was Elvin the third, according to what Vera had explained earlier.

It was one of the first times in a while since she'd seen Elvin. He looked a bit disoriented as if he hadn't quite gotten over his hangover. He flew in this morning from New York where he had been on another "business" trip. He was taking a drink with some associates.

Bianca sat with her mother-in-law and some of the other rich housewives.

The sun shone brightly overhead.

The course looked fun, with a faux tunnel and tiny little ramps that included a water obstacle with water bubbling up from golden custom-built fountains.

"Make sure you pass everyone else in that course, baby," Bianca coached Evie from the side. "Keep ahead in the game, don't fall back. Speed up if you see anyone gaining on you."

Evie pouted.

"Evie," Vera added. "Your mother's right. Keep ahead. Keep focused."

They were preparing her for the life she would lead, Penny supposed.

What ever happened to just having *fun*? Was Evie even allowed to have fun for the sake of it like normal kids? She would have plenty of time to be a grown up later. Childhood only happened once.

In the race, Evie was ahead for a while, only to be overtaken by Veronica from the Maximiny Cosmetics family who raced past her and eventually won. She could feel the angry energy and disappointment coming from the Wingarden camp. Penny hoped they wouldn't make Evie feel bad about not winning.

"Evie was in the lead. What happened?" Elvin shouted.

Bianca pouted and folded her arms across her chest. "She messed up."

Elvin frowned.

Penny was willing to bet they'd placed a bet on the race and lost.

Vera's fury was so ridiculous it was hilarious as she spoke with one of her high society friends beside her who came to lend support.

"Evie should have won. But she had no chance against that little sugar doper," Vera said to her friend, trying to save face with no shame. "That's why Veronica won. My precious little Evie never has any artificial or refined sugar in her diet," she huffed.

Sugar doper? They were accusing the three-year old winner of *doping*? *Seriously? You have so got to be kidding me.* Their precious little Evie never ate artificial sugar or candies? *That's* why she lost?

Penny resisted the urge to roll her eyes. Penny wanted to tell them to get over it. They were three-year-olds for crying out loud.

Still, Evie didn't seem bothered as she sipped from her cup full of cold, refreshing water.

"Evie, you did amazing! Congratulations, you came in second place," Penny finally said to Evie when she approached her family. It looked as if her parents or grandmother weren't going to say it.

"Okay," Evie said quietly.

"No. It's not okay," Bianca snapped. "Never accept second best Evie. You will do better next time."

Penny felt a surge of fury race through her. Was she serious? Okay, Penny, it's her daughter. Evie's only your charge. No one said anything to Penny's defence and she was utterly gobsmacked. This was not an easy job to say the least. No wonder Evie had issues though she was only three. She wanted to tell Evie it was all about having fun and being happy for everyone else.

Penny could feel the heat of Bianca's glare.

"You know something, she's right," Vera's friend finally said nodding to Penny. "Penny's right. It's a game. And she should be proud where she placed. She did her best. Better luck next time."

"I suppose." Vera said, not convinced.

They really were full of themselves.

She was glad the race was over, but it looked as if the parents had a harder time with the outcome than Evie.

But one thing was for sure. And it was a very dangerous revelation about her new employers.

The Wingardens hated to lose.

25. Bianca

The following day, Bianca made her way to the west wing. She was still not over her daughter losing the Bakeroo cup. That was supposed to be her moment. What happened? And that little bitch Penny speaking out of turn like that. She would show her.

"So what is this about?" Bianca asked.

The family had gathered in the grand living room by the marble stone fireplace and rows of bookshelves. The butler had just served refreshments.

Mr. Stephen Liivon, one of the partners of Liivon, Liivon & Spence, the law firm handling many of the Wingarden family affairs was present with one of his lovely young secretaries.

"Please have a seat, Bianca," Vera said, her tone flat.

Elvin sat by his mother, saying very little as usual, a drink in his hand. What else was new?

He gave Bianca a polite nod.

"I'm glad you're here, Bianca," Mr. Liivon said. "I was just saying to your mother-in-law and your husband that everything should be in place soon as per Elvin the second's last will and testament. But Evie will not receive fifty percent of the estate on her fourth birthday which is coming up soon."

Bianca felt sick to her stomach. "Oh?"

"We've decided at our discretion to postpone it until she turns at least five years old. At which point she would receive fifty-percent in trust to help with her care and upbringing and the rest when she turns twenty-five."

"I see."

The family still had access to money. She knew that.

Why did her belly tighten with knots all of sudden? Were they planning something without her? To leave her out of some deal?

Why wasn't she invited to the meeting when it all began?

"I'm sorry, I had no idea you were even meeting today." Bianca tried to sound polite.

"Well, we know you have a lot on your mind, dear. We don't want you to feel overwhelmed."

"Overwhelmed?" Bianca was offended.

"Yes, dear. You know, ever since your pregnancy and the birth, you've had a bit of trouble coping, you know, with Evie."

And whose fault was that? Putting me through hell when I was pregnant. Forcing me to do these horrible paternity tests to prove Evie was a Wingarden?

"I don't understand."

"Well, as you know," Mr. Liivon continued. "Elvin the second wished to leave his entire fortune, his shares in Wingarden Department Stores and all his assets to his grandchild. That would be Evie. And, he felt that the estate would be better left to his grandchild to be overseen by a board. Now because Evie is underage, she would require a trustee. Ordinarily, it would be her parents, but..."

"But what? Why can't we be her trustees?"

"Well, dear, my son's former gambling addiction has the board feeling uncomfortable. Elvin is dealing with his issues. And with you and your..."

"And my what?"

"Well, your depression, dear, and your erratic spending. We just feel it would be best if I take full control of Evie's financial affairs."

"What?"

"I feel that..."

"I heard you the first time. I meant what the hell are you thinking? I'm Evie's mother. You can't just use me like some rent-a-womb and expect me to just sit back and do nothing else."

"But you haven't been doing much else, except the gardener." Elvin downed the last of his drink.

"What? What about you screwing every dress around town including that stupid dog walker, Flora. What about that? You think I don't know what you've been doing in your *meetings*? Everyone could hear through the walls. It's not like the basement with the sound proof wall."

"Oh, come on, Bianca. You tricked me into marrying you by getting pregnant." He ignored her last statement.

"The last time I checked, it takes two to get pregnant. Do your math? Oh, I'm sorry, I almost forgot. You're bad at math and every single subject at school. It was your *daddy* that paid someone to take your tests for you."

Elvin's face reddened.

Vera gave Bianca a scathing look.

The lawyer looked embarrassed to be there and held his head down pretending to shuffle his notes.

What had Bianca done? She'd kept her cool this whole time. She kept her tongue when they were insinuating things about her. But this? She could not afford to lose any of this. Not now. She worked too hard to come to this point.

Vera looked aghast. She then regained her composure and cleared her throat, eyeing the lawyer as if to say, 'See, I told you she's unstable.'

Bianca collapsed on the leather plush chair in the grand living room.

"I'm sorry," she said quietly. "I was...I..."

"It's all right, dear. We know you're under a lot of stress. That's why we have Penny here taking care of Evie for you. Don't worry, while she's here you can just focus on getting better. I think Penny can stay on for as long as Evie needs a nanny. She seems like permanent material."

"Oh she's wonderful," Elvin agreed to the lawyer.

"Yes, I've heard good things about Penny the super nanny." The lawyer chuckled then stopped when he saw Bianca's face.

Bianca's eyes widened.

Were they really serious? Did they think she was expendable, just because she was having issues? And whose fault was it? Living under schedules, stupid rules and contracts. This was a family, not a freaking *institution*.

Never mind that damn app Vera gave her. The Evie's Mom app. How damn crazy was that?

Vera was a control freak. A crazy person. And now she wanted to get rid of Bianca so they could control Evie and the fortune that old man left to her.

No wonder he didn't leave anything to his widow or his wayward son. Vera was right about one thing though, it was Elvin's money. It certainly wasn't his godawful personality or lack of ambition. No wonder the older Elvin wanted him to have none of the fortune to squander at a casino.

Bianca did them a favor by providing an heir or all of it would have gone to charity. Every last penny of it.

Elvin the second wouldn't have been the first billionaire to leave his estate to no one in the family. They were lucky he said, if he had a grandchild, he'd leave it all to him or her. And how did they thank Bianca? By planning to get rid of her?

Evie was half her blood. They couldn't get rid of her that easy.

26. Bianca

Bianca had to have another plan. She had to get rid of that stupid nanny who was making her look bad. Then she'd figure out what to do about the Wingardens.

The following day, she sat at one of the most expensive private restaurants in the area, serving only members of the club with Daphne, her old friend.

Daphne was ever the reliable friend. The only friend from her past.

The waiter had just left the table after taking their order. They both ordered the lobster and shrimp special with baked potato.

Elvin used to take her to lunch there too, but not anymore. Not since Evie was born. She'd done her part to provide him the heir the family needed. They couldn't care less about Bianca and quite frankly, she couldn't care less about them either. As long as she was getting her allowance and the gifts, she was good.

The guilty gifts were the best.

Whenever Elvin would return from his trip from New York or Europe or out west, no doubt with whomever he was grinding between the silky sheets of his bed, he'd return with diamonds or a designer bag to add to her massive collection. Each gift, each diamond, each bag was a reminder of his infidelity and his cover up. Then she'd show it off on social media about how spoiled she was as a rich housewife and he'd look good—and so would Bianca.

She was beginning to get a bit tired of the charade. She glanced down at her sparkling diamond. Well, not that tired, she grinned to herself.

"It's gorgeous," Daphne said.

"Thanks."

"What's on your mind? You seem far away."

"The Wingardens hate me."

"What? If those are a symbol of hate," she said pointing to Bianca's diamonds on each of her fingers. "I'd love for them to hate *me* too."

"It's not funny, Daph. It's all a show. It's a front for them to look good in the public eye. To look as if things are going great for them and they treat me well." She was careful not to say too much about the company's finances as per the signed non-disclosure agreement with Vera.

"No seriously. It's all in your mind, B."

"I don't think so," Bianca said, defiantly. "I really think they're trying to replace me. You should see the way they look at Penny, as if she's some sort of freaking super goddess or something. It's annoying."

"But she is looking after Evie and you said she's good with your daughter. Besides, why would they try to replace you? They can't. You're Evie's mother. The rich don't like to part with their money, honey. I know that all too well. They know full well it'll cost them an arm and a leg to get rid of you."

"But what if they try to lock me up or something?" *Or worse. What if they try to silence me mob style.*

She didn't trust family institutions like that. She'd better be careful.

"Lock you up?"

"Yes, in an institution. You know Vera's been hinting to Elvin to have me see a shrink or something for my postpartum depression." She frowned, sipping her wine.

"Oh, right, I've heard that one in three women who give birth can suffer postpartum depression up to three years after giving birth."

"I guess I'm one of those statistics."

"But that's not your fault. You had a rough pregnancy."

"I know. Especially during the latter part of the pregnancy after she forced me to do a paternity test."

"Yikes. She's the loving mother-in-law we all want."

"Tell me about it." Bianca took another sip of wine. Her second glass.

"You sure you're okay?"

"I'm good. It's just that..." She rubbed her fingers over her tattoo.

That crazy new nanny kept eyeing Bianca's forearm as if she knew Bianca from somewhere. That was going to be a problem.

The more she thought about it, the more she felt uncomfortable.

Bianca searched her brain trying to remember if she'd seen Penny anywhere in the past. She couldn't recollect.

Bianca wondered if Penny and she had a run-in in her past. A long time ago.

But if so, that was a long time ago. Why would she want to work for her now? Was she trying to get back at Bianca for something she'd done? The past was dead and gone. She'd moved on now. She was a completely different person now. She wouldn't hurt a fly—not intentionally anyway.

Self-defence was another matter though. If someone threatened her or her family, she'd stop at nothing to protect them. That was a whole different matter.

Bianca knew being the richest housewife in the country meant you had a lot of haters out there who'd love to see you fall like a bad stock on the market. Well, that was not going to happen while she was alive and kicking. And she'd kick anyone's ass who tried to mess with her or her child.

Still, Bianca's mind went back to Penny's expression when she first saw Bianca's tattoo.

What if the nanny knew about her background? Would she go to the boss of the household, Vera? Vera would gladly get rid of Bianca in a blink of an eye—if she knew the truth about her real past.

Bianca would have to stop Penny. She was going to put a stop to it once and for all. There was no way she as giving up her carefree life. No way in hell.

27. Penny

Penny was late. She had to get to the west garden for the garden party which started an hour ago at three o'clock.

The Wingardens sure hosted a lot of events for the heads of a cash-strapped corporation.

Still, her time was running out. She'd been there close to ten days now. And it felt like forever. She knew she had to make her move soon with Evie if she was to get her money back. They were going to fire her. She knew it. That was their sick game. But she wasn't leaving without her money. No way in hell.

Bianca had told her that the garden party was at four o'clock. Why would she do that? She uploaded the information on her Nanny app and the time read four o'clock. Then Penny received a call from Vera asking her where she was since Evie was running around wild on the lawn with her little friends, the children of the distinguished guests.

"I'm so sorry, Vera. The Nanny app said the garden party started at four." Penny was breathless by the time she reached them on the massive lawn.

"Are you sure?" Bianca said, with mock concern in her voice.

"Yes." Penny took out her phone and opened the app. She then slid her fingers across the screen where the party was listed.

Shit.

It read three o'clock on the app now!

Vera read the screen of the phone. "It says it starts at three o'clock, dear."

"But..."

"Maybe you should see an optometrist. You might need some new reading glasses. My friend couldn't read the fine print on her phone either, even when she enlarged the font." Bianca's tone was mildly sarcastic.

Penny wanted to scowl. But she resisted.

"I'm so sorry. It was a misunderstanding."

"Never mind, dear," Vera said. "You're here now."

She didn't bother get into the fact that Bianca had asked Penny to re-organize Evie's doll collection while Evie had her piano lesson. It was a set up. But that's okay. She knew when her cue was coming. She'd be out of there in no time. And Bianca would know exactly who she was and she would have to give her back her money.

The garden party had tons of who's who in society. Top lawyers, industry professionals, pro athletes, some super models and businessmen. It was an event the Wingardens put on from time to time, including a fashion show with proceeds going to charity, of course.

Bianca was with her society friends taking selfies for her social media page.

Evie was playing in the doll house. Some guests came over to ogle the record-breaking life-size doll house, taking snapshots.

When could Penny be alone with Evie? This might be her moment. Her chance.

But then when she looked around and saw the waiters and servers dressed in white tuxes walking around the grounds offering refreshments and wine to the guests and the security discreetly roaming. She realized it might not be as easy this time.

Penny had fun playing with Evie and her friends. They pretended she was a life-size doll and did her hair, sticking ornaments on it while Penny pretended to be a talking doll. She even did a little dance for the kids.

It was quite a show. In all honesty, Penny was enjoying the carefree time. She was reminded of what it was like to be a child again. Laughter and playing. That's how childhood should be, not competitions, or in Penny's case, wondering if you were going to eat that day or go to school in dirty clothes where the kids would laugh at you.

She noticed the expensive clothes the kids had on. All name-brand stuff they'd soon grow out of. She wondered if the parents would be donating the clothes to a children's charity or clothing kids who didn't have new clothes or proper clothes.

"Bravo!" one of the guests laughed and clapped. They began to take pictures.

Penny grew nervous. Did she really want them taking pictures? Would this show up on their social media feed? They really should ask her permission first.

Later, Vera approached Penny in the study. "Penny, you have a wonderful way with children. They all loved you. You're like the Mary Poppins of Sun Valley."

"Hey, it's my job."

"Oh, no, dear. It was above and beyond what you did today, letting the children play with you like a grown rag doll. Oh, how delightful. And you allowed them to paint your hair. They were so happy. You are doing very well here. We're very pleased."

"Thank you," she said.

Penny noticed Vera twirl her pink pearl earrings in her ears. They were a gorgeous pair.

"I love your pink pearl earrings."

"Thank you, dear. These were given to me by my late grandmother. God rest her soul. She received these as a gift from my grandfather during the Victorian era. These are my lucky earrings."

"They are? Beautiful."

"Oh, yes. I love to wear them when entertaining. Pink is my favorite color."

"Mine too. They're gorgeous."

"Thank you."

She noticed that Vera loved her pearls. So far she'd seen her wear golden pearls, ivory pearls, lavender pearls and black pearls. Unlike Bianca who was dripping in gold and diamonds every day.

Just then she saw Bianca outside the door to the study near the marble staircase. Was she listening outside the door? She felt a chill come over her. She didn't trust Bianca. That tattoo. She shouldn't have been looking at it too hard. Would Bianca suspect her? That she knew about her past?

28. Penny

"Is everything okay, Ma'am?" Penny asked Vera the next day as she noticed Vera's frantic expression in the hallway.

Penny was on her way to the poolside where Evie would be having a party with her friends.

"I'm missing my pink pearl earrings."

"Oh?" Penny swallowed hard, her stomach tumbled inside her. "Where did you last have them?"

"Yesterday."

"Um."

"I thought I placed them in my jewelry box last night."

She looked carefully at Penny. Did she think Penny had something to do with it missing?

Shit!

It was just yesterday Penny was commenting how beautiful they were. If she didn't know any better, she'd swear that Bianca had something to do with it. But she couldn't say that could she?

"I hope you find them soon, Ver...I mean, Ma'am."

"I hope so too." Vera continued on her way, crestfallen.

Penny felt deflated now. She'd woken up in a good mood so this was a heavy mood swing.

Just then Elvin walked by. "Everything all right, Mother?"

"No. My pink pearl earrings are missing."

"Oh, no. Not the ones your grandmother gave you?"

"Yes, those ones, my lucky pair."

Bianca stepped out of her Shoezeum hearing the commotion in the massive corridor. Another staff also came to her aid. "Did I hear correctly, Ma'am? You lost your pearl earrings?"

"Yes."

"You know something, that's funny because I'm missing one of my pear-cut diamond rings," Bianca said.

"You are?" the maid said.

"Wonder what could have happened?" Bianca cast a suspicious glance at Penny.

Penny's breath stopped. She wanted to say, why don't you look in the mirror for the answer, bitch! But she decided to keep her tongue.

"I'll be at the pool side with Evie now. I hope you do find it soon, Ma'am," Penny said, gently.

She said nothing to Bianca.

Penny sat at the poolside in her T-shirt and jeans like the good nanny, because wearing beachwear wasn't appropriate with the husband of the house around. That had been one of Bianca's unwritten rules. She probably meant it wouldn't be appropriate with the hot young gardener or other workmen around.

Bianca was the Queen Bee around there. She had to be the adorable center of attention. No one else.

Vera later left to go on a boating cruise though she was not happy about misplacing her earrings. She told the staff that she probably misplaced them, but Penny couldn't help but feel that she might have a suspicion that Penny could have taken it, which was not true.

Hopefully the water would calm her nerves down a bit.

Later, Penny's mind went back to Vera's pearls. She really hoped they would show up somehow, though she doubted it.

At least the day-cruise on the lake would take her mind off of everything.

29. Penny

A day later, everything seemed frosty around the Wingarden household since Vera's missing earrings. Penny had to make her move soon. She sat in her room, thinking.

Bianca was after her and now she wasn't sure if Vera trusted her, thanks to Bianca.

She'd been so sweet to Vera, but Vera seemed a bit icy towards her now. It had taken her so damn long to get Vera to warm up to her and now it looked as if she'd slid back to sub-zero degree temperature in her personality.

Bianca was dangerous.

Penny could believe that Bianca tricked Elvin into marriage by getting knocked up. She'd heard that Vera had her do a prenatal paternity test. Who could blame Vera? Bianca was lucky it was Elvin's baby.

Still, she seemed tricky. No rich guy's going to just go having babies with random women knowing a paternity suit could cost them hundreds of thousands.

Right now, Penny needed a way out. Ten days were up now. What if the loan sharks found her? She was supposed to get her money back from Bianca and leave the country. That was her plan.

The crooked loan sharks who were after her late husband and who were now after her, needed payment or else. She was sure they were calling to harass her on her old cell phone, but since she didn't have that phone in her possession as per the agreement with the Wingardens she had no idea of the messages they were leaving her.

She needed to get her money back from Bianca.
And she was going to do it.
But the question was how?

30. Penny

Later that evening, after dinner in the grand dining room, Penny took Evie to get washed up and ready for bed. The Wingardens were entertaining the Chaletrins that evening. They had a full-course meal to entertain people they tried to impress to let them know the Wingardens still had it, despite stock reports and changes in the market as they tried to compete with the online retailers.

The Wingardens Department Store chain was founded in 1906. Those were the days. It was the in thing back then. But sadly, not all companies could keep up with the changing times in the new millennium.

Later, she went upstairs to Evie's quarters and helped her put away her massive doll collection. The kid had fun messing the room up, but no one taught her how to put her toys away when she was done. Penny did that, to Vera's pleasure.

Well, at least she was happy then, but clearly Vera was still unsettled about the missing things from her room including her precious pearl earrings and now Bianca had claimed to have missing things too.

Well, she was willing to bet Bianca was behind it all. Looks were deceiving. The family had issues. Maybe having more money meant less trust of people around them. Who'd want to be so paranoid?

They seem to be using the girl as a prop to their crazy lavish lifestyle—their meal ticket.

And it was time for Penny to make a move on their meal ticket.

31. Bianca

Bianca glanced at her screen. Some shithead sent her a text message from an unknown number. What the hell was this about?

Some people would do anything for money.
Peniaphobia is the fear of poverty,
fear of being broke, fear of being poor,
fear of having no money.
Fear of not being able to survive.

What?

Was this some sort of a juvenile joke? Vera must be behind this. It had to be her. Or was it that bitch, Penny. But why would she send this? And her phone would be tracked. She wouldn't dare send her a text like this. Unless she got a friend to do it. No, it had to be Vera. She'd been calling her a gold digger for ages now. That bitch Vera. She was on her last legs and she had no idea what Bianca had planned for her.

Bianca sat on the edge of her plush four-poster bed and got up when she heard a knock at the door. It was the butler.

"Sorry, Mrs. Wingarden. The contractor is here about your balcony."

"Oh, thank you. Please send him in."

The contractor walked into the room looking around. Everyone had that reaction when they walked into Bianca's massive elegant boudoir with the French doors. The marble stone fireplace was the centerpiece. To the side were multi-paned glass French doors leading to the veranda which faced the west garden.

The contractor made the assessment and then came back into the room.

"Just as I thought. It's an old building. The balcony will need to be replaced. Might take a few days and there'd be tons of work and dust."

"Oh, that's no problem. I can...I mean my husband and I can stay in another bedroom during that time."

"Good. In the meanwhile, you might want to stay away from the rail."

"Of course." Bianca was delighted to hear that the railing was very unstable.

Later, she walked down the spiral marble staircase toward the study where she would be having a family meeting with Vera and Elvin. Every time she had a family meeting, she didn't know what to expect. She hoped it would be to fire that crazy nanny. If not, she had other plans.

She always had a plan B.

"We've seen that you been unfaithful," Vera said later in the meeting. "You're clearly not happy in your marriage. You have a difficult time coping with Evie and ..."

"Wait. What? We're having this discussion again?" Bianca said.

Vera sighed deeply. "Dear, we only want what's best for all of us. You see, I've had the lawyer draft up an agreement. We think it's best for a separation and then a divorce. You will agree to our terms."

"I don't think so!" Bianca shot back.

"Or you'll get nothing." Vera's tone had an air of finality to it.

Did she suspect Bianca of taking her precious binder that day?

"Nothing?" Bianca echoed incredulously. "Are you both crazy? I can and will take half of what's mine."

"Half of what, dear? As per your prenuptial agreement, if you cheat on your husband, you forfeit anything in the divorce."

"I haven't been unfaithful. You can't lie about anything in court."

There was no way they could prove she'd slept with Grant, the gardener.

Just then Grant came into the study, looking embarrassed. Did Grant tell them? Did that SOB talk about what they'd been doing in the garden shed?

"What's going on?" Bianca said to Grant. "Why are you here, Grant?"

"My name's really Rod, I'm a friend of your husband."

Bianca's jaw fell to the floor.

"What? You fucker. You set me up!"

"I had to. I can't afford any trouble in my life," he pleaded. "I'm sorry, Bianca."

"What are you talking about?"

"I think that's best, dear, that we end this amicably for the public and for Evie's sake."

"You can all go to hell. I'm going to bring you all down."

The hell she was going to let them take her daughter from her. They were not going to use her. They got what they wanted didn't they? They got an heir that could collect the billion that old man Elvin the second left behind the money he was going to leave to charity instead if he didn't have a grandkid.

It wasn't over.

Not yet.

Bianca stormed out of the study. She could not believe this. They were willing to push out the mother of their heir? Just like that? Just dispose of her like she was nothing. That was just plain wrong.

Shit.

If Bianca cheated, she got nothing. And what did they get? The kid? The heir? Their nest egg?

That old miser left everything to his granddaughter Evie, not to his wayward son or his wife, apparently. He had an iron-clad will. Very disturbing dynamics. She began to wonder if having this kind of wealth was worth the pain. You met all kinds of crazies. She'd read where a billionaire left absolutely nothing, zilch to his own child.

Nada.

Money was a strange thing. It bewitched people. No one talked about what they had in the bank. And who could blame them? People changed when it came to money. It was a survival game. You needed it to survive. To buy food, water and shelter which weren't free. And those were the basics for human survival. And it was costing more each year to survive.

Inflation was outstripping salaries. No wonder some people lived off credit to eat.

She thought about that text message she received earlier. Was that Vera's crazy way of stalking her? Vera was playing head games with her. She never did think she was good enough for her stupid son, Elvin.

There was no way she would go back to being poor. No way in hell.

32. Penny

This was it.

Penny had to make her move now.

She'd been listening outside the door of the study when it all went down. She could not believe her ears. This family was more insane than she'd imagined. They were on to Bianca and had set her up?

Still, they did not know the half of it. If they knew the crime Bianca had committed, they'd call the police now and have her locked away.

She should not feel sorry for Bianca. She brought this all on herself. She hated the way the Wingardens behaved, but she could not feel sorry for any of them.

Bianca stole my money.

She stole my life.

Her late husband's loan sharks would bury Penny alive any day now. They'd showed her husband what happened when clients didn't pay up and what they'd do to their family.

She had to get her money and skip town. Penny was going to get her money back from Bianca. They were getting rid of her—but she needed to get what she came for.

Moments later, she received a text message on her Nanny App from Bianca to meet her in her bedroom. It was luck that Bianca asked to see Penny in her bedroom. That was a strange meeting place, though. Why in her bedroom?

She told Penny she wanted them to have a chat with her on her balcony.

Penny thought nothing of it.

The massive balcony was beautiful and had a lovely reddish brick floor, two patio chairs and a table with a plant and tea candle on it. Must be romantic in the sunset. It overlooked the verdant west garden you could see the lake in the distance and the trees. Breathtaking. Must be nice to wake up to that.

She'd never been there, she'd only seen Bianca, presumably it was Bianca, standing by the window looking down at her while she played with Evie in the garden. Perhaps she'd been watching to make sure she was doing a good job with her daughter.

"Us women have to stick together, Bianca," Penny told her after they'd had a little chat and Bianca vented to her about her troubles.

She was surprised that Bianca opened up to her after all this time. "I'm on your side."

"What? You're on my side."

Penny nodded.

"Thanks. I thought you were on *their* side," Bianca said, with a fake sob as she dabbed tears that weren't there.

"I'm on the *right* side. Let them think what they want. Don't worry, I've got your back."

"It means a lot to me to hear you say that. Family is nothing but trouble. You know you don't speak much about your family," Bianca added.

"There's not much to tell."

Bianca poured Penny a drink and told her she had time to listen.

"Well, I had a husband, but he...he passed away."

"Sorry to hear that. So you never had children then?"

"I did."

"You did? I thought...I mean I heard you couldn't have children."

What she probably meant was that she was listening in on her conversation with Mel that day when she said she couldn't have kids, Penny thought to herself.

"I had a baby," Penny said. "But...I lost her...it was for the best. My husband was involved in some shady stuff I knew nothing about at the time. We lost our home, our savings and the loan sharks came back and said they'd get payment from me."

"That's terrible."

"Yes. It is."

33. Bianca

"What happened to your baby?" Bianca asked as the two ladies sat on the balcony as the breeze blew through their hair. She was glad to be getting along with Penny. All this time, she thought she was her competitor, but she was her friend. Maybe she'd misread Penny.

And to think she was going to push her against the faulty railing and make it look like an accident. But maybe she could run off with Evie and take Penny with her.

No, that was crazy. The Wingardens would never let her do that. Besides, she still had to get rid of the nanny. Just like the last one. Then maybe Vera would see that they needed Bianca to take care of Evie.

"Well, I was at the hospital," Penny said, "I didn't have much money. My husband had been killed in a so-called accident and so I had to make do. He was hit by a drunk driver."

"Sorry to hear that."

"It's okay. I think it could have been the loan sharks sending a message. They knew he had some money somewhere. I had no idea where. He was involved in some shady stuff to do with properties and what have you."

Bianca listened attentively, wondering when would be the best time to shove Penny off the balcony.

"Anyway, I contemplated leaving my baby in a foster home until I got a job or something or got my life back together. You know temporarily," Penny continued, "but then that decision was made for me. Something happened and I accepted that maybe it was a way out."

"I thought your baby died?"

"No, but I got a way out."

"A way out?"

"Yes. You."

"Me?"

"Yes. You see, here's what happened. My ex ran up a lot of debt. Real estate shady deals. He drank too much. He cost me a good job. I fell pregnant. Then he was killed. I was left with an unborn child unsure of what to do next. We were counting on that money to pay the mortgage. Lost the place. Had nowhere to go. Literally. Slept at a bus shelter. Then went to the hospital to have the child but do you know how terrible it is when there's no one to visit? Nowhere to go afterwards. I thought about leaving the hospital without the baby, but I couldn't. I was depressed. I prayed for an answer. Anything."

"What happened?" Bianca probed.

"A young woman dressed in hospital scrubs that did nothing to hide the hideous red rose tattoo on her forearm came and took her when I was in the bathroom, but what she didn't know was that I had spy cameras in the room. I felt sick to my stomach to come out and see the baby gone. But what could I do? And since I was confused and thought my prayers were answered because you took her so carefully, I thought I'll just walk out quietly out of the hospital with the empty car seat while the nurses were in a meeting and don't say anything about a police report. I knew I had your face on camera and could go any time to the police. Anyway, when I googled you and saw you were married to a goddam Wingarden heir, I thought. Shit. My baby lucked out. But of course, she's mine. I had to watch over her. I saw that you were pregnant before but it looks as if you lost your baby somehow. Only by following you did I know what happened."

"You're crazy. You can't prove that." Bianca was breathless. Her heart raced with fury.

"Oh, but a DNA test can. That's some charade. Looks as if he only married you once you had a live birth."

"You've lost your mind. Evie's *my* child."

"No, you've lost *your* mind. You lost your mind when you lost your newborn at the roadside by highway 4—your golden ticket. Your way into the family fortune. It makes sense, you told no one and just fucking walked into a ward and like any sane person you thought, what the hell, I'll just *snatch* someone else's newborn."

"You're crazy." Bianca was paralyzed with shock. She could not move. This was not happening.

"By the way," Penny continued. "Her real name is not Evie."

"What?"

"I named her *Money*. Yes, my daughter's name is Money. That's what I called her when she was born. Because growing up we never *had* any money. I wanted to make sure my little girl wouldn't want for anything. So maybe she could live up to her name, it could bring her good luck. And I see it did in a strange way. I knew the name Money could mean something. I couldn't care for her when she was born but I kept thinking about my Money. Money was on my mind. I thought day and night about Money. Where she was, if she was cared for, loved like I wanted to. I knew I would come back for her one day. I might not have been able to protect her or care for her then.

I was too weak, but I never stopped loving my Money. Money is my daughter. Or whatever you call her. She's my Money. You had my Money and I wasn't leaving without her. And I would do anything for my Money. Anything. In fact, when I get her back, we're leaving town so that no one finds us."

Bianca froze.

"By the way, just a heads up for next time, if there is a next time, if you're going to sport such an in-your-face, unique tattoo like that, you should be a law-abiding citizen because it was so easy to track you down. You thought no one saw you take Money, but I did."

Bianca's blood ran cold. Her entire body went *numb*.

Bianca said, "I overheard you say you couldn't look after your kid. You were weeping in the room. You couldn't even afford diapers. You were talking to someone on the phone about walking out and leaving your baby. I thought it would be perfect. I would give her a perfect home. You never called the police, so I knew I did the right thing."

"You're sick. So what if I was depressed? I just lost my husband and everything. And had no money, but I wasn't going to really leave her. Yes, I didn't bother call the police because I thought for a moment that the universe was giving me a break. A way out until I got back on my feet. I thought you were a social worker or something. I...I...I want my Money. She's all I have. I stalked you first to make sure you would take care of her. But you're just using her for the inheritance. You don't even care about her."

"Neither did you. You needed a way out. You were going to leave your baby."

"No, I wasn't."

"You think going to a shelter after the hospital with a newborn was a good idea?"

Penny flinched.

34. Bianca

Bianca Thomson gazed up at the sky which had now turned a deep shade of red. The color of blood, like the blood stains on her fingertips and her hands. Like the blood red rose tattoo on her forearm.

Her pulse pounded in her throat. She didn't have much time as she pulled up to the oak tree by the dirt road. This would be the perfect spot. No one ever came there.

Her hands were covered in blood, her shirt, her pants. She would have to change them soon, but first thing was first.

She turned off the headlights and shut the engine off. Moisture pooling on her face, her anxiety overruling her body. She glanced around nervously. No cars were driving by. It was an isolated area. The sound of crickets sounded in the background. Nothing else except for the heavy fast beats of her heart.

Terror.

She'd never done anything like this before. Her chest heaved. Anxiety ripped through her. It wasn't supposed to end like this. The day wasn't supposed to end like this. Why did it have to end like this? Why?

She'd never hurt a fly before, much less another human being.

She needed the money. She couldn't help it. She needed a way out.

She got out of her vehicle. Blood was everywhere. She'd have to clean the blood later—clean away all evidence.

Her breathing was labored as she popped open the trunk and saw the body lying there. She gagged. She squeezed her eyes shut. She couldn't bear to look at the lifeless body. It wasn't supposed to end like that. The blood stains on the face, the eyes, the nose, the neck.

Horror gripped her. She would never forget the face. It would haunt her forever.

She grabbed the shovel and made her way over to the oak tree. She'd have to dig a grave as deep as she could to bury the body. Bury the evidence. Bury the past. Bury the pain. No one could ever know. She didn't know how she was going to keep this to herself, but she would have to. Her life depended on it. Her freedom depended on it.

She glanced around again. It was a good thing it was out there in the country, a wooded area where there were no cameras. Everyone had hidden cameras everywhere in the city. It was as ubiquitous as having a cell phone.

It took longer than she'd thought to dig into the dirt—and more laborious. She wiped the sweat off her brow. Her muscles burned. Her lungs ached. Her back was on fire.

Bury the body deep, like the memory of this event at the back of your mind.

But in her heart she knew nothing stayed buried forever. But she would deal with that later. Even if that would mean looking over her shoulder, watching her back, every waking moment of her life.

It was a mistake. It wasn't supposed to happen like this.

She then grabbed the stiff body, dripping with blood like her hands. Heavy as the weight of guilt on her shoulders.

She swallowed hard and placed the body in the makeshift grave, looking around, glancing nervously over her shoulders.

"Sorry," she whispered to the lifeless body. "I'm so sorry.

No one could ever know about this.

Would karma catch up with her?

She would wipe this day out of her mind forever, like the ghost of the past. *It was an accident*, she justified in her mind. *It wasn't murder. It wasn't planned.*

But hiding a body *was* a crime. At the very least, it would insinuate guilt.

Would anyone ever find out what she did? Would they understand? She had to make sure the pit was deep enough so no one would ever find the body.

If anyone found out what she did, her life would be over.

She was a criminal. But she needed money fast. She needed money.

She glanced at an old newspaper clippings.

Nanny for the super rich. Jobs available now.

Nanny kidnaps child in her care and sells on the black market for $800,000.

She read the article to see if they were going to give details on how it was done. The child would not be harmed, only given to parents who needed a child.

She then knew what she had to do. She was going to get a child. She was going to take someone's newborn and pass it off as her own. They'd already forced her to do a paternity test while the baby was in the womb. They wouldn't do another one once the baby was born, would they?

It was Vera's fault. That stupid bitch never wanted her precious son to be the father of her unborn. So what did she do? She forced Bianca do the unthinkable and have a risky in-utero paternity test, prodding the fetus with a needle. Damn it.

Bianca had cramps in her belly ever since. It didn't help that she smoked dope. She helped kill her baby, didn't she? But she was under so much pressure and scrutiny from Vera, the bitch.

She was through with being poor. Elvin told her his father was leaving everything to the baby. Billions of dollars. Nothing to them. But the baby died inside of her. She wasn't about to let that money go.

Bianca had met Elvin the third at the nightclub, they'd hit it off. She'd lied about being on the pill, of course. She'd been ovulating so she had it all planned out, her window, his weekend of passionate guilt-free sex, cheating on his girlfriend. Well, she got pregnant. Taking fertility pills helped. She was not going to be broke and looked down on ever again.

Then his mother called her a gold-digging whore. Well she was not. She was valuable. She carried the Wingarden heir. They needed one soon or the old man was going to leave everything to the Bookmanship Library. They would have none of it. Heck, Elvin couldn't even read. His daddy paid for his education and paid for people to take his tests for him. His mother knew that. He was no good and his daddy didn't want to leave money for them. Stupid Vera said Bianca and Elvin the third could only get married *after* the baby was born *live*.

Born live?

Imagine that.

Well, the baby was still-born thanks to stupid vile Vera, but she wouldn't have the satisfaction of knowing that. If they found out the baby had died, Bianca would lose everything. Everything was dependent on her having this heir.

Bianca was not giving up.

She glanced at the article again. No, she would not give up. She would go into the hospital with some scrubs and head to the maternity ward. She'd made sure of it.

This stuff happened all the time, didn't it? She could do this.

But first she had to bury the evidence, the dead fetus she just gave birth to. She would pretend she gave birth on the roadside. Which she did. The doctors would concur. She would just have to get a substitute baby. She was going to marry Elvin Wingarden III and give him that valuable heir one way or the other.

35. Penny

Penny had it all planned out from the beginning. She knew who had taken her baby. She knew where she went, what job she had, who she was married to.

Poor Elvin seemed like a very nice man—odd and imperfect, but nice, nonetheless. And his wife duped him for his money. Gave him someone else's child to secure an inheritance.

It took Penny three years to find this gem of an opportunity to get close to the Wingardens and she'd done many jobs including volunteering at the women's prison as a drama coach, taking a job as a receptionist at a private detective agency where she learned a lot, but then her most useful job had been at that elite nanny agency.

She could never wipe the memory of the arms that took her baby. That horrible, massive red rose tattoo on the arm of the kidnapper who'd stolen her Money.

Her precious baby daughter named Money.

She'd suffered massive postpartum depression and couldn't care for her and wanted to leave her there after her husband was killed. She felt hopeless. Helpless. Alone.

It was a good thing she knew Bianca hired from the elite nanny agency thanks to her social media feed. And it was a good thing that Penny got a job for and was working at the agency and when the call came it, she placed gorgeous nannies in a pile along with her homely self, hoping the Wingardens would take the bait. And they did! She was in. She got a way in to see her Money. Her daughter.

"Have you heard the term peniaphobia?" Penny asked. "I studied about it in abnormal psychology."

Bianca gave her a blank stare. She could see the wheels turning in her head of what to do, but she was paralyzed with shock.

"Peniaphobia is the intense fear of poverty, fear of being broke, fear of being poor," Penny continued, "fear of having no money. Fear of not being able to survive. For some people, the fear is so intense they will stop at nothing to avoid it. Like you. But as the saying goes, be careful what you wish for. Your spirit, your instincts, the ones you often ignore like the one telling you it was wrong, you ignored it.

"Just as it was telling you that you should be fearful of me. I saw the way you would look at me as if you recognized me or as if you should know me. People should trust their instincts more, you know."

"You're a psychopath. Are you going to kill me?" Bianca said, backing away slowly toward the patio sliding doors.

"It depends on what you mean by the word kill. Do you mean physically or emotionally, like what you did to me when you kidnapped my newborn baby? Do you know my breasts ached? It wasn't just my heart that ached with longing for my baby, it was my breasts that ached because they were so full of milk and I couldn't do anything to relieve them like feed my newborn, because you'd stolen her, you bitch!"

"You're a crazy woman!"

"You see, I needed this job. It had everything I needed. I would have room and board, a decent salary, food, and most importantly, I would get my daughter Money back."

"You can't prove that I stole Evie from you. Listen I...I..."

"No, I'm not a crazy woman. That would be you, Bianca. And I can prove a thing or two. I thought about going to Vera, but then she has a vested interest in the inheritance tied to Evie and I find her a little creepy. I knew she'd probably hear my story and then have the family's fixer bump me off and cover up the crime. You know like a hit and run."

She could see Bianca looking at a way to get back at her. Bianca's eyes kept darting to the balcony rail.

"You see I've held many jobs since college," Penny continued. "Odd jobs, but as my grandma once said, all jobs have value. You learn from people. Even driving cabs, you learn about people's habits. Life. What interests them. We're here to learn, right? Well, I worked for this agency as a receptionist. A detective agency. The guy had all sorts of spy cameras. Including this little one here. The watch. It has a built in camera. See? I placed it above little Evie's head when you snatched her. I caught your face on camera. Later, I used Google Images and was able to link you to your social media account. And well, I knew who you were and I tracked you to the oak tree where your little one was buried. And well, you know in order to cope with what you did until I had enough strength and courage to face you I had to go along with my little plan and pretend that your daughter was mine and I went to her grave to visit her. I couldn't sleep at night knowing my daughter was with a kidnapper and I wasn't doing anything about it yet. So it all worked out. I waited almost four years for this moment."

"Four years? You were planning on befriending me, gaining our trust. My trust."

"Yes, I'm a patient person. I waited for the right moment. I never knew it would take four years, but it paid off. I knew you used Elite Nannies and I waited for the moment when I would wiggle my way into your life. You have everything out there on social media. It wasn't hard to figure you out. What you do. What you like. Who you use. It's all there for me. It's so easy to spy these days. People leave a trace of their secrets everywhere online. Even filming the birth of your baby. Of course the video cut off at the actual birth. That's because you knew something was wrong. But you still had good evidence that no one would suspect that Evie wasn't yours. People saw you push something out. You already had the in-utero paternity test, as you've said before. It all seemed to work out."

"You're sick."

"Yes, I lost it when you stole my baby, my daughter Money."

Bianca's eyes widened with horror. Her penciled brow had a terrified expression on it like a silver-screen era actress during a scene of fright or terror.

Her breath was halted. Who could blame her? She didn't know what Penny could do to her now. Her world was about to fall apart.

Penny stood by the rail of Bianca's bedroom balcony.

"You bitch!" Bianca screamed.

"No, I'm not a bitch, but karma is."

"You won't get away with this!"

"You stole my baby." Penny's voice was hoarse now. "My grandma would always say, Penny, be careful what you do because the unseen eyes are watching you. That's the mighty one, the universe, karma, whatever you call it. We're always being watched, even if you don't realize it. Did you really think you were going to get away with it?"

Suddenly, Bianca teared up. "It's my mother-in-law's fault." Her voice was shaky, tearful, raged.

"What?"

"I was pregnant with Elvin's fucking child and she made me prove it by sticking the baby with a needle to do a paternity test. They couldn't wait until the baby was born to find out. That caused me to have a miscarriage."

"I'm sorry to hear that. But you shouldn't have used my baby as a replacement. You stole my baby, my daughter, Money."

"You....you s-stalked me and premeditated this? You knew this whole time and never went to the cops. You tried to snake your way into our lives? You're a goddam psychopath."

"You have the heart to call me that? You lost your baby and instead of going to your sugar daddy and fessing up, you decided to steal my child to pass off as his so you could keep your gold, you whore."

"You'll tell no one. I'm going to silence you," Bianca screamed and charged at Penny, lunging forward with rage in her eyes.

Penny's heart pounded hard in her throat. She moved just in time and Bianca crashed into the balcony, smashing through the railing.

Shit!

The loud piercing scream could be heard everywhere.

Penny heard the horrible thump sound of a body hitting the ground. She glanced over the rail-less balcony.

Bianca was on the ground, a pool of blood over her head, but she wasn't moving, her head was snapped back.

Shit.

She was dead!

Penny stood frozen to the spot, overcome with a deep state of shock.

36. Penny

Penny didn't know how long she'd stood frozen there but moments later then she heard the sound of steps coming up behind her. Elvin crashed into the door of the bedroom and ran out onto the balcony.

"I....I...I'm so sorry, sir. I don't know what happened," Penny said, breathing hard and frantic. She didn't mean for this to happen. What would happen now? Would they have her arrested? She was going to have to come clean with him.

"She jumped, didn't she?" Elvin said. "She was really depressed," he said, looking more relieved than shocked.

Then Penny remembered the family meeting they had with Bianca earlier. They were planning to get rid of her, weren't they? Were they the reason the balcony rail gave out so easily?

He had a drink in his hand. What else was new?

"I've called the police," he said, his voice cold as ice sending shivers of fear down her spine.

Did he really call the police? She didn't like the way he said it so calm and cool. There was something in his eyes she didn't like. Something she hadn't seen before.

Hate.

She had a feeling the wrong psychopath was lying on the ground over the balcony.

Before she could do anything, he punched her and she blacked out.

When she woke, she was in the room in the basement. The soundproof room with cement walls. The cellar had once been a storage area for coal, required for open fires and to heat water back in the Victorian era, but it wasn't really in use now.

Elvin had tied Penny to a wooden chair. She couldn't move. There was a Persian rug on the floor nearby. Other than that, the room was cement all around. No windows. A small light overhead.

He explained that he had to do this because no one could now about their little ruse. Then he started off on a rant about his now dead wife and his overbearing mother as she had no choice but to listen. Her cheek still ached from the blow from his fist.

Seemed as if he needed to get a lot off his chest. Why did criminals feel the need to just ease their mind and spill it out to those who they think would never be able to talk about it? To clear their conscience and get it off their chest? Was the burden too heavy? Everyone needed an outlet of some sort.

Her smart watch was recording everything. Thanks to her Goth friend, Dee, at the market. She'd given her a useless-looking watch that happened to be a smart watch. One that could record and didn't rely on Wi-Fi. She'd seen one before at her old job at the detective agency.

He left the room and came back some five minutes later.

"What are you going to do to me?" she pleaded with him when he came back into the room. "I won't say anything. It's just that..."

"You tried to kidnap my child?" he scowled. "You're going to stay here while I call the police," he said. For the cameras, obviously. He was using his cell phone to disable all the cameras in the home while he spoke. To cover himself, obviously. No wonder the house was quiet today. They'd probably planned this whole thing out, but it worked better than they had anticipated with Bianca dying the way she did. The house had no staff on duty tonight, she noticed.

Shit.

What was he going to do to her? Assault her?

"No. You've got it wrong. I...your wife kidnapped *my* baby. She's mine. I can prove it with a blood test."

"I know."

Penny froze, her heart stopped beating.

"You know?" She spoke slowly. Her voice quivered.

"Who the hell do you think put her up to it?" he said.

Oh, God. She was in the soundproof room in the basement. No one would hear her scream.

Never trust anyone with a soundproof room.

Who the hell needed a soundproof room? And why?

What was she going to do now?

What was he planning to do to her? Cement her in the basement as he probably did to his previous late wife who couldn't bear him children.

She was stuck. No cell phone. His home. No way out. No windows. He was six foot four inches. Broad shoulders. The battery on her smart watch hadn't been charged in a while and would probably run out soon.

"So you were the one that scarred her wrist?" Penny said, trying to buy time. Trying to stall him, keep him talking, allow him to incriminate himself for her watch. Whatever battery juice she had left.

"Yes, I like to leave my mark on my women."

"You're a sick bastard."

"I try my best. Too bad no one knows about it."

"Bet your father did. That's why he cut you out of the will."

Her eyes darted around the room, but she shouldn't have taken her eyes off him. Before she knew it she felt the pain from the hard slap of the back of his hand. His ring cutting into her cheek.

Shit! Pain shot through her body. She looked around the room.

"Oh, there's no escape," he said.

"That what you told your first wife?"

My watch is a smartwatch. Everything you've said is being recorded.

As if he could read her mind, his eyes drew to her smart watch she'd gotten from her friend Dee.

"What the hell is this? I hadn't noticed it before. It's not on the list of approved accessories."

"Approved accessories?" Penny tried to move her wrist from his grasp but it was too late. He ripped the watch off her.

"You fucking bitch. You were recording this. You breached the agreement."

"Breached the agreement? You just assaulted me, asshole. There is no agreement."

Her pulse raced. Her eyes widened with despair.

He slammed the watch down and smashed it into the ground stomping it with his foot.

"So you were recording this, hoping to track me?"

"No. I..."

She was toast now. That was her only hope. Would he, could he erase the confessions on the watch?

Just then the doorbell rang and he answered it with his cell phone.

It was the Flora, the dog walker. She came running down the stairs in the basement.

Maybe she could appeal to Flora.

But when she came downstairs, Flora just glared at Penny.

"Meet my first wife, Lauraine," Elvin said. "Plastic surgery looks great, doesn't it?"

What the...?

"I don't get it," Penny breathed, breathless, her heart pounding hard and fast in her chest.

"My crazy father left nothing to me except a dollar. And everything to his biological grand-child. Well, Flora wasn't able to have any children of her own and I wasn't going to be left out. You know he told my mother to make sure the grandchild was his, so we couldn't even adopt a child. They wanted the Wingarden bloodline to carry on or they'd cut off all money. So I went to the club where gold diggers hang out, looking to trap rich, unsuspecting men. Yeah, you think I don't know what those bitches are up to? I figured why not get one of them knocked up. They were willing. Only they won't live long enough to get child support or alimony. Two can play that game."

"You're sick."

"Who do you think told that stupid bitch to grab a kid? My father was dying and refused to change the will unless I came up with a biological heir. Then Bianca told me she lost the fucking kid. I told her to bury it and told her to get another one so the old man wouldn't know. My mother already had Bianca's in-utero paternity test done. They wouldn't test again."

"You're really sick. You need help." *And twenty-five years behind bars.*

"And Flora, don't trust him. He...he'll do the same to you too."

Flora just continued to glare at her. "You'd better keep your mouth shut. He's got a mean-ass temper."

Penny's jaw fell open. She could not believe it. The woman was as sick as he was.

So Bianca wasn't his wife then. His first wife was still alive. This was a scam. An elaborate scam.

So he got money from his first wife's life insurance policy. That's how they managed to stay afloat until the inheritance came through.

Was Vera in on this too?

Both Elvin and Flora tightened the knots on Penny's wrists. What were they going to do to her?

He took out a carving knife and began stroking the sharp blade gently. "I love to make my mark on skin. It's beautiful."

"You did that to your wife? You're the one that scarred her?"

"Yes, and I had her get another rose tattoo to cover it up. Too many people were asking questions about her wrist. A little hard to cover up. I told her if she ever told anyone about the abduction, I would say it was her idea."

Penny's eyes widened with shock. She could not believe what she was hearing.

She had it all wrong this whole time.

Elvin was behind it all.

She'd overheard Bianca telling a friend someone had looked at her diary and searched through her things.

Penny asked Elvin about this.

"Yes, it was me. I knew I couldn't trust her. I knew Bianca wasn't her real name, well not her original name anyway, just like I knew who you were from the start. Who do you think had you followed?"

"So it was you? You had someone follow me on the bus on my way to the interview with you?" And all this time she thought it was the loan sharks from her late husband's dealings.

"I had to know who the finalists were, didn't I? People always lie on their resumes."

"I don't believe it."

"I have a lot of men working for me. You need to have a lot of ears and eyes around if you're going to be a man in my position. You see, you bitches are not too bright. I was behind it all, the games. Even stole my mother's precious earrings, the pearl earrings she loved more than she loved *me*," he grunted still toying with the knife.

"So you took the earrings? Your mother thought Bianca stole them. Then she thought I stole them."

"Yes, it was me. I couldn't have you all trusting each other or forming some sort of alliance against me. I had one of my men hawk them for some more money. You know, you can never have enough money. Waiting for Evie's inheritance was taking too long. I hated that they put it off until she turns five. And even when she turns five, it won't be the full amount."

"You're a sick person. All these nasty games."

"Boy, I've always loved games. And you know the funny thing is that my father never thought I was too bright. But he was wrong. I played everyone like a game of chess, right into my palm. God, you guys are all stupid. My daddy was wrong. I'm not the one who was stupid."

"You have some serious daddy issues," she said quietly.

She watched as a vein pulsed on his forehead.

"That man was a loser," he said, grinding his teeth with anger, "He was a bully. I hated everything about him. He never cared about me. Only his damn money. I can't believe he wouldn't leave a penny to me. I gave him time. Made sure he got to spend time with Evie before his untimely death."

"You had something to do with that too?"

"He was taking too long to die. I did him a favor. Sped it up a little. I knew he was dying so I just helped him along."

She wiggled to get free but it was no use.

"You'd better let me go."

I knew your little scheme," he said ignoring her comment. "Don't you think I would recognize the eyes? Evie has your eyes. I figured it was you, but I knew I could use you for your purpose. You were too dangerous to let loose. Keep your friends close..."

"And your enemies closer," she finished for him.

"That's right."

She was dead. She knew there was no way out now, but she had to keep him talking.

He moved the carpet that was on the dirt floor by the cement wall. There was some sort of trap door and when he opened the trap door there was a large square hole on the floor. Some sort of coal chute in the ground. Or was it a storage tunnel? Either way, it was a large dark square hole. Large enough to shove a few people in and no one would know.

Who knew how far down it went.

And who knew what was else was in there. Or *who* else...

"What are you going to do?" Penny said, her heart pounding fiercely in her chest.

"Bury you alive, like the last nanny. She tried to blackmail me, that gold-digging bitch. Good thing Bianca got her to confide in her. Bianca told me what her plan was. She tried to say she was pregnant after I forced her to have sex with me which was a lie. Bianca told me all about it. I told everyone that she drowned on the yacht, but she didn't. She's down there."

My God! Bianca lied about that nanny. She set her up. She set her up to be killed by Elvin.

"I knew that nanny's child wasn't mine. After Evie...well, after I got Bianca pregnant, I had the accident. I couldn't have any more children after Evie—after the child Bianca was carrying for me. That's why it was so important to still let my father think Evie was mine, or else I would have lost everything. The whole fortune."

Her eyes widened.

"No one would ever find you. It's a deep, dark tunnel. It was built during the early 1900s when the mansion was constructed. It's like a bottomless pit. But it hasn't been in use for a while."

He pushed her chair further towards the edge of the large square dark hole. She could see nothing down there but rocks that seemed to go down forever. She would crush her head going down and die instantly if he tossed her in there.

"No!" she cried out. "Please! No!"

But it was no use.

Penny squeezed her eyes shut and started to pray. She'd never prayed before in her life. Never believed in it. But she was desperate now. She squeezed her eyes shut tighter, tears streaming down her face, her heart thumping wildly out of her chest.

Just then, she heard a shoving sound and she heard Elvin and Flora scream out and two large thumps, the sound of bodies hitting a ground.

She opened her eyes and turned around.

Elvin and Flora had vanished.

They were gone.

But Vera was standing there at the edge of the hole staring down, her chest heaving.

"What? What happened?"

"He was no good. A murderer!" Vera's teeth were clenched. "He...he...he killed my dear husband, his own father. He's getting his just rewards now," she said. "And I can't *believe* he stole my pearl earrings."

Holy shit! She killed Elvin over her husband's death *and* her pearl earrings.

Memo to self: *Never* borrow jewelry from this woman.

Penny never heard Vera coming. She must have snuck down the stairs and was listening in the whole time. Thank God, Vera was a sneaky little snoop who crept around and spied on people. Thank God for *that*!

"I don't like scandal," Vera continued, untying the rope around Penny. Penny wanted to add, you don't like scandal but you're okay with murder? But she was just happy to be free and *alive* right now.

"The Wingardens' good name and reputation is all we have now," Vera said. "It's all we have."

Did Vera just push her son and first daughter-in-law into the pit they'd dug for Penny, into the grave they'd made for that other poor nanny?

"It's one of the laws of life," Vera said. "If you dig a hole for someone else, be prepared to fall into it yourself."

If you dig a hole for someone, better make one for yourself too, Penny once heard her late grandma say.

Well, it looked as if Elvin learned that lesson the hard way. As the saying went, he had too much money and not enough cents—or sense.

Still, Vera pushed her son and his first wife into the pit, but she did it to save Penny's life.

37. Penny

It had been a month since the news broke about the Wingardens' missing heir Elvin the third. Vera took ill and spent some time at a psychiatric ward at a private hospital. She ended up confessing to what she did and was under the care of a psychiatrist. No wonder. Poor Vera. Her son killed her husband. She killed her son. And the granddaughter she thought was hers turned out to belong to the nanny. So she went from having an affluent family to no family at all. That would be enough to make anyone lose it.

Would criminal charges come later? Penny had no idea as yet.

Vera had sought to have Penny take charge of the child before falling ill since she was already the live-in nanny and had built a rapport with Evie.

Later, a blood test was done, and because Evie was a minor, all the information was not made public.

Penny drew in a deep breath as she sat in the law office of Liivon, Liivon & Spence. It was the right thing to do. She had to tell the lawyer the truth. And so she did.

He paused when she finished.

Her heart pounded hard in her chest.

He looked at her. His gaze holding hers. What was he thinking? Was he going to call the police? Tell her and Evie to go away and never come back?

"Look, Penny," he said, pulling his glasses off his face and resting them on the oak table beside his files. "Mr. Wingarden knew Evie wasn't his grandchild."

"What? But how...he died not knowing."

"He looked into her eyes and saw her hair and knew she was probably not his. But oh, did Evie give him the biggest smile and hug he'd ever received in his life. He loved her so much and told me that she was to get everything in trust on her fourth birthday should she survive and that the rest of the money when she turns twenty-four. So that her family couldn't squander it all. Of course, he gave us power to change the inheritance dates at our sole discretion and we decided age five and twenty-five would be better for each installment. Anyway, he hated that his son and daughter-in-law deceived him, but family meant a lot to him and Evie gave him something no one else did."

Her heart pulled. Tears misted her eyes. "What was that?" Her voice was soft.

"Unconditional love. That's what kids give you. They are born innocent, trusting and loving. Hate is something that is learned. Evie knew nothing about hate and deceit. And as he always said, family isn't always blood, it is those who are loyal to you, protective of you. And that's the kind of bond they had during her first year before he passed on. He had so much pleasure hearing her giggle and tug on his tie. He loved her and didn't care that she was not his. He left everything to Evie, not to his grandchild. To the child you have with you now."

He looked troubled for a moment. "Now, let's get this straight. He had no idea that Evie was acquired illegally. He assumed that his son used his name and got a quick adoption of some sort. It was a good thing he didn't live to see what an even bigger disappointment his son had been." He sighed deeply. "So half her fortune will be bequeathed to Evie as planned when she turns five. Thank you for your honesty. It's pleasing to know that Evie will be in good hands," the old gentleman said.

Penny was overcome with emotion. She could not believe it.

Yes, Evie will be in good hands.

38. Penny

It took four weeks after her death before Bianca's funeral could be arranged. That was too long, but Bianca with the twenty-million followers had a beautiful service.

Penny stood there after the flowers were placed on the grave, wearing a black dress and a large, black-rimmed hat that covered her eyes and her bright red lipstick. She looked like a rich widow.

She held a single red rose in her hand. Like the tattoo that had identified Bianca like a trail leading to her treasured child, to the answers to her miracle.

She found her.

She found her daughter. She should have gone to the police. She knew she took a chance. It was luck that worked out this way because the Wingardens could have gotten rid of her.

One day, she'd tell Evie she was her real mother, but not now. Let her have her joy.

Everyone commended Penny for her great care of Evie and how wonderful it was for her to stay on. Little did they know that when enough time passed, the truth would come out.

A grin curved Penny's luscious red lips. Mother to Evie Wingarden. That sounded nice. Or, as she was called at birth: Money.

Penny grasped the rose and held it to her. When everyone else had walked away, she turned her head slightly to see if anyone was watching her.

Then she spoke softly.

"I'm sorry it had to end this way, Bianca. I find it ironic that you had a tattoo of a red rose with thorns on it. Thorns are supposed to symbolize loss, and thoughtlessness and in the tarot world the rose is thought to be a symbol of balance, beauty, promise, hope, and new beginnings. Isn't that funny? Well, this rose in my hand, like the red rose tattoo that led me to you symbolizes a new beginning for us both. What you did was awful, taking Money or Evie from me, but then she wouldn't have this life and I wouldn't have the life I'm about to have. I hope you find the peace where you are now that you never found here."

She then placed the rose on the grave.

This was a new beginning for them both.

If this were a movie no one would believe the coincidental events, but truth was sometimes stranger than fiction.

Evie would be just fine. She'd inherited a substantial fortune from her adopted granddaddy Mr. Wingarden of the Wingarden dynasty, all in her own name.

She was going to be all right. She was going to be fine. And they were going to have a good roof over their head and food in their bellies and everything they wanted. But most of all, they would have each other.

Penny was going to pay off Rexton's debts so they would leave her and Evie alone. And she was going to make sure to give back to the community to which they came from.

Karma did have a way of evening the score for those who've been wronged.

Later, Penny and Evie played at the park. Evie didn't seem to miss her other mom much, since they rarely spent time together.

Bianca had spent more time with her Yorkie than her own daughter, maybe because Evie wasn't her real daughter. Who knew?

Penny was happy. She was truly happy seeing her daughter laugh, happiness glowing from her heart and bright smile as if no care in the world. That made Penny happy, seeing her daughter happy and healthy. She was going to donate all her rich clothes to the poor kids when she outgrew them.

Whoever said money couldn't buy happiness was wrong. It's the good money could do that brought the sunshine in a smile.

Penny felt warm inside as she looked lovingly towards her daughter who played with Porsche, the Yorkie, on the grass, laughing and enjoying her moment.

Yes, life wasn't just about material things, it was about precious moments with your loved ones to cherish for a lifetime.

Penny would do anything for her Money, her beloved three-year old daughter named Money.

***

Thank you for reading The Rich Housewife. If you enjoyed this book please leave a review at your favorite retailer to share your experience with other readers.

Books by Ann-Marie Richards

Missing (A gripping psychological thriller with a shocking twist you won't see coming)

The Rich Housewife (A gripping psychological thriller with a shocking twist)

About the author

Ann-Marie Richards enjoys the things in life that are free like spending time with family and cherishing every blessing. She has a degree in Psychology and enjoys reading and writing about matters pertaining to the human spirit. She loves to read mild psychological thrillers with a twist, powerful love stories, romance and mysteries. She is thrilled to hear from readers. You can send her an email at annmarierichards.author@gmail.com

Lightning Source UK Ltd.
Milton Keynes UK
UKHW010742060223
416537UK00003B/952

9 781393 263500